Secrets of the South

B.M. Hardin

Hardin Book Co.
www.hardinbookco.com

ISBN 13: 978-0-692-18372-4
ISBN 10: 0-692-18372-8
LIBRARY OF CONGRESS CONTROL NUMBER: 2018913220

Author Email: bmhardinbooks@gmail.com

Publisher Email: hardinbookco@gmail.com

Printed in the United States of America

Dedicated to Shannon

Secrets of the South

CHAPTER ONE

No one ever told us that *hunching* was wrong.

In the south, that's what we called grinding our bodies up against each other with clothes on, before the age of ten.

And surely playing 'mama and daddy' was even worse.

We just didn't know any better.

All we knew was that days and nights were hottest at the end of July. And that running in and out of the house made grandma's light bill go up; at least that's what she said. We knew that the one pitcher of water, on a hot summer's day, was never enough to go around. And that the creek behind the old church was the closest thing that we had to a swimming pool. We knew about doing laundry in tin buckets and hanging clothes on every door of the house to dry. We knew that house keys weren't necessary because no one ever bothered to lock their front doors. And we knew that having sex before marriage was the quickest way to be labeled a whore.

That's what the South is to me.

The South is memories.

Pain and agony.

The South is…me.

I started to feel nauseous as I drove down the gravel driveway towards the plantation house.

I haven't been *home*, to Clover, South Carolina, in about fifteen years. I'd fled the small town the day after my high school graduation. I'd left with nothing but the clothes on my back, a small stash of cash and an even smaller amount of hope.

I remember that day.

I remember running.

I remember the sound of the old screen door slamming shut behind me as I ran out of the house in tears. I remember having my tiny purse in one hand and all my important papers in the other. I remember running up the gravel driveway and all the way to the dirt road. I just kept running. I ran past Mrs. Hilda's old house and with her old dog Bo running behind me, I ran until I reached the main road. I remember telling Bo to go back home just before sprinting across the highway to the crowded store.

The Hop Stop.

To this very day, the store was still there. And just as busy as ever. I'd driven by it just a few minutes ago, and just like back then it was still right next to the old used car lot.

$1,139.45.

That's how much money I had in my purse on the day that I ran away. The old car lot had a 1990 used Honda Accord that I'd been saving up for. It was $1200. I was almost there. It had taken me two whole years of babysitting, running errands, and braiding hair to earn money, but *that* day I didn't have enough. So, I had to change my plans.

I approached a random woman just as she finished pumping her gas. I offered her fifty dollars to take me about forty-five minutes away to the Greyhound bus station. I didn't know her; which was a surprise. In this small town, everyone knew each other, with a few exceptions, but I had never seen her before. I figured that she was probably from one of the small cities on the other side of the state line. Since our town was so close to North Carolina, folks were always crossing over to take advantage of our town's cheap gas.

She was a complete stranger, but that day she became my angel. I never asked her name, but she agreed to take me to the bus station, after explaining that she was going that way anyway. Thank goodness we were living in a different time back then and that she hadn't turned out to be a crazy person because without thinking twice about it, I got into her car and I never looked back.

I didn't know where I was going once I got to the bus station. I just wanted to get there. I didn't know what I was going to do. I didn't know what would happen to me, but I figured that it couldn't be anything worse than what I'd already been through. It couldn't be any worse than what had happened to me here.

I never planned on coming back here.

I never even wanted to.

Yet somehow, here I was.

After a life full of success, love, and then divorce, I was right back where it all started. And I was looking for something that I'd been struggling to find anywhere else.

I was looking for inspiration. My story.

I was looking for my voice. My next breath.

Once the woman dropped me off at the bus station all those years ago, I'd looked at the list for hours trying to decide where I wanted to go. I hadn't been anywhere outside of North and South Carolina. We didn't travel much when I was growing up. And whenever we did go somewhere, it was never too far and always somewhere that we could drive to get to.

I stood there and tried to remember places that I'd heard about before or places that I'd seen on T.V. And then I heard the lady over the intercom saying that a bus to Walla Walla, Washington would be leaving in just a few minutes. Instantly, I remembered reading something about their community college. My life had been full of havoc and heartache, for months, up to that very moment, but I figured that if I was starting over then college was an excellent place to start on my new journey. I was eighteen, and I could do pretty much everything that I needed to do on my own, so I took a deep breath and paid for a ticket to catch that bus.

So many hours, and five bus changes later, I stepped off the bus in an unfamiliar place, but for the first time, ever, I felt free.

I felt alive.

And I knew that I, Savannah Louise Lynch, would do whatever I had to do to survive.

I walked alone to a twenty-four-hour pancake house that was nearby. I stayed there all night, eating pecan pie, drinking black coffee and looking through the newspaper from the day before. Once the sun came up, I made my way to the closest bus stop and found my way to Walla Walla Community College.

And my journey to a better life began.

With the help of one of the advisors, I applied for financial aid and enrolled in summer classes. They offered housing assistance, so after staying at a hotel for a little over a week, they helped me find a place to live. I snagged a job at the 24-hour pancake house, and slowly everything fell into place.

I pursued a degree in Communication Studies and all alone, all on my own, I obtained my associate degree. I didn't have any family or close friends there to see me walk across the stage, but I didn't let the feeling of loneliness stop me. Instead, I headed to finish up my studies in the Big Apple.

I headed to college in New York, at NYU, where I got my bachelor's degree; and that's where I've been ever since. Currently, I live in Manhattan.

After college, I landed an internship at a flourishing publishing company, and then I advanced to an entry-level position where I excelled beyond expectations. I did my job so well and so efficiently that I found myself continuously being promoted until eventually, I became Editor in Chief.

And the position had its perks.

Honestly, I loved it, and I hadn't imagined that I would ever want to do anything else---until my life was turned upside down.

Until I felt pain.

My divorce from my ex-husband, Nathaniel, was hard on me. It changed me.

Nathaniel had always been a fantastic husband. He was so good to me, but I hadn't lived up to his expectations. Truthfully, I hadn't kept up my end of the deal. We got married only a year after knowing each other underneath the evening sun in Spain. We were so happy, but after about five years in, Nathaniel was ready for me to deliver on the promises that I'd made to him.

He wanted kids.

He wanted a family.

The family that I told him I would give to him, but it never seemed like the right time. I was too busy. I was thriving in my career, and I told him to wait.

I guess he got tired of waiting.

We argued about it for a long while, and after finding my stash of *the morning after* pills, Nathaniel asked me to choose. He asked me to take a break from work and pick us; just for a little while, but I refused. And in the end, I had to deal with the repercussions of making the wrong choice.

Nathaniel left me, divorced me, and now he was having a baby with some Persian woman named Nada. It wasn't until after I lost him and after he moved on that I started to see my job and my life in a different light.

What's the point of success if there's no one waiting at home to tell you that they're proud of you?

Being an editor was rewarding, but I suddenly had the dying urge to be on the other side of the pen.

I wanted to write.

11

There was something that I needed to say. A story that I needed to tell; whether it was my own or one that was make-believe. I just had to get it out.

So, I started trying to write my first novel, only something was missing. Honestly, it was missing a little bit of everything.

I knew what I wanted to say, or at least some of it, but I couldn't seem to find the right words. I didn't know where to begin. I didn't know how to start.

So, I had to give it all up.

I resigned from my position and told my former employees; the people that I'd grown to know and love, that the next time they saw me, I would have a book submission and I would be looking for a publishing deal.

Money, for now, isn't an issue.

I have plenty of my own *and* some of Nathaniel's. I figured that I would have a book in circulation long before I ran out of funds.

If only I could write it.

And then one rainy day, I stood up from my desk; the one that's placed directly in front of the bay window of the two-story brick home that Nathaniel and I once shared in the suburbs of Manhattan. I closed my eyes, and it was as though something deep down inside of me told me what it was that I needed to do.

I needed to run.

It was time for me to run away---again.

Not for good this time. Just for a little while.

And so, I did.

In a hurry, I packed my bags, and after grabbing my laptop, I headed out my front door. I got into my car, and I just started to drive.

New York wasn't where I needed to be.

I needed a change of scenery.

For three days, I drove from city to city, state to state, looking for somewhere to nestle in for a while.

Somewhere to connect and reflect.

New Jersey. Pennsylvania. West Virginia.

None of those places had what I needed.

What I was looking for just wasn't there.

Is it here?

It can't be here.

Right?

Never in a million years did I think that *here* was where I was going to end up.

I stopped in front of the old plantation style house.

The house had been in my family for over a hundred years. It had been given to one of my great grandfathers' in the 1800's, as a gift from the family that used to *own* him.

Generation after generation had lived here. I can remember a point in time where about ten family members lived in the house at the same time. It was the one place that any of us could always call home.

For me, this house had always been my home.

It was the only place that I'd ever lived as a child.

And it was one of the reasons why I'd gone away.

Now, my grandma Whinny, my great-grandma Deloris, who we all called Gamma, and my Uncle Willie, were the only ones who lived here; at least they were the last time I spoke to my cousin Marlo.

That was about two years ago.

I didn't talk to my family much.

I never really had much to say.

I never got to meet Gamma's husband; my great-grandpa since he'd died long before I was born, but my grandpa Bobby, who had been Grandma Whinny's husband, died a few years ago. That was the last time that I'd heard from grandma.

Grandpa Bobby had been one of my favorite people growing up, but still, I didn't come home for his funeral.

So, what in the hell am I doing here now?

I remember Grandma Whinny calling me for the first time in years to tell me the news and to share his funeral arrangements with me. She'd somewhat demanded that I show up.

I didn't.

Maybe showing up here now wasn't such a great idea.

She never called me again after that, and that was years ago. And if I didn't know anything else, I knew that grandma knew how to hold a grudge. She was probably still pissed and upset with me.

Uncertain, I put my custom all-white Audi into the park gear. It had been a gift from Nathaniel, just a few months before he left me.

I glanced around the crowded yard.

Instantly, I started to feel overwhelmed by the sudden flood of childhood memories.

The old house sat shamelessly on a few acres of land. The run-down barn that used to house chickens and an old horse we called Smoke was still standing across from what used to be a cotton field.

Growing up, we'd never had any close neighbors.

Mrs. Hilda's ancient house had been closest to ours, and it was about a three-minute walk up the dirt road, after walking up the long gravel driveway.

The garden that I grew up tending to with grandma was massive now. That woman had a green thumb if nothing else and she'd always been able to make anything grow. I was too far from it to see the exact goodies growing in it, but I could only imagine that it was a little bit of this, a little bit of that, a little bit of everything.

The old tire swing was still tied to the big oak tree in the front yard. It had been there long before I was born. It was even in some of the old pictures that

Gamma had of Grandma Whinny and her siblings when they were younger. I couldn't help but smile as I remembered that sitting right there was where I received my first *real* kiss.

It was from Jace.

Jace.

I haven't thought about him in years.

I shook my head as I opened my car door, refusing to entertain thoughts about my first love. Before entirely getting out of the car, I spotted the buckets by the well.

Grandpa Bobby's old truck was parked a couple of feet away from it, and with the grass growing up around the tires, it was safe to say that his truck had probably been parked right there, in that very spot, since before he died.

A heart attack was what killed him.

Probably from the years of fatback, pork chops, pig's feet and everything else that grandma cooked and fed to him.

Finally, I stood up and closed the car door behind me. I continued to look around. I continued to remember.

One nagging mosquito unceasingly hovered around my nose, forcing me to take my first step. The rustling leaves of trees attempted to comfort me as I inched closer and closer to the front porch.

It was early fall, and the leaves were starting to turn.

I wasn't sure if anyone would be happy to see me.

I'd been told time and time again of how much of a disappointment I was for turning my back on my family. I'd been preached to and verbally chastised over the years, whenever I would answer the phone. Eventually, everyone stopped calling.

All of those years ago, I called Grandma Whinny from Walla Walla, the same night I arrived. I'd used the phone at the pancake house. I called her because I didn't want her to think that I was dead. She asked so many questions. Most of them I couldn't answer. I just told her that I was okay and that I was gone. And that I wasn't coming back home.

After that, I didn't talk to anyone from here for years. And then with the age of social media becoming a thing of popularity, it wasn't long before I became reconnected with family and childhood friends.

And once I gave my phone number to my cousin Marlo, she gave it to everyone else, and the calls of judgment and disapproval started to pour in.

I remember hearing grandma's voice, for the first time, after about five years. The tone of her voice had changed drastically; as though she'd aged in dog years. She rebuked me for disappearing, and she told me that she didn't understand.

She didn't have to understand.

Leaving was the only way to save me.

It was the only reason that I was still alive.

I made my way up the crooked and cracked porch steps.

For some reason, in my head, I could hear Gamma's raspy voice calling me 'white girl'. That's what she used to call me when I was younger.

My skin was lighter than most of my relatives, but mama always told me that it was because we had a little bit of Indian in our blood. Every black person I knew often claimed to be related to Indians, but for us, it was actually true. I'd never met any of them, of course, but I'd seen old pictures of them.

Still, I was teased for being light-skinned and for having prettier hair, but only by my family. Everyone else outside of my inner circle seemed to be intrigued by my appearance and natural beauty. It was safe to say that some of them were probably jealous, but I didn't understand why. I would've killed to have just a splash of their melanin in my skin any day.

My skin was a combination of buttermilk and honey, and I had a head full of big beautiful curls. I was always very petite; which had been something else for them to torment me about.

"Savannah, where's the rest of your ass?"

They would say.

"Why are you so damn skinny?"

They would tease.

"Girl you need some meat on 'them' bones."

I used to eat like crazy, hoping to gain weight just to fit in. I never could. And to this very day, I was still a little on the slim side. The only difference now was that I had spread just a little in the hips and with age, I'd gotten just enough junk in my trunk to hold onto. It was enough for me, but I'm pretty sure it still wouldn't be enough for them.

The steps creaked until I made it to the top of them.

Two old wooden rocking chairs were on the porch, along with a table that held a vase of fresh daisies.

The porch used to be my favorite place.

It was so big. It wrapped around the entire house. From one side to the other. I'd spent so many summer nights on it with a good book and a blanket, or sometimes I would just lie on it, with a pillow and look up at the stars.

I noticed grandpa's unfinished projects.

It looked as though he'd started refurbishing and painting the front porch railings, but he never finished. And no one else had bothered to finish up for him. His tools and cans of paint were still sitting on the porch, covered in dust and cobwebs. Obviously, no one had touched them in years.

As I stood in front of the front door, I started to sweat.

I was sure that the door was unlocked. All I had to do was turn the knob. The people down here never locked their doors.

Ever.

Then again, times have changed.

The world was so different now.

For a second, I almost changed my mind.

What are you doing here, Savannah?

I'm not sure.

All I had to do was turn around and walk away. That's all I had to do. I could go back to my life. I could go back to peace and back to pretending that they weren't there. I could go back to acting as though my family didn't exist. I didn't have a husband to go home to anymore, but I could find someone new. All I had to do was take a step back and turn around but...

I didn't.

Instead, with a shaky hand, I turned the doorknob.

Unlocked.

I stepped over the threshold into the house.

And as soon as I was inside, I was reminded of the day that my mama died.

Well, the day that I found out that she was dead.

My mother was murdered, but before I had a chance to entertain the thoughts of her I heard Gamma's hoarse voice.

"Well, I'll be damned," she shouted.

I stood in the oversized living room, too far away to see the actual expression on her face, so I inched closer to her.

"Little white girl, is that you?"

"Yes, ma'am. It's me."

"I reckon it is, huh! Well, come here chile, so I can get a good look at ya'," she barked.

I haven't heard good ole' country talking like this in years.

Gamma had to be about ninety-something.

She'd outlived most of her children, and she probably had a few good years left before she kicked the bucket.

The mean ones always take the longest to die.

She stared at me, rubbing the nub of her right leg. According to Marlo, she had her leg from the knee down amputated some years back. It had something to do with her diabetes, but diabetes couldn't even take her old ass out.

"Did you bring yo' white husband wit' you girl?" She asked.

I merely shook my head.

Marrying a white man, Nathaniel, had been like the end of the world to them. I couldn't say that they were racist, but they'd been raised during a different time. A time where their memories weren't the fondest of white folks, and they didn't believe in mixing the bloodlines. You couldn't bring another race home to meet them---at all. They just wouldn't accept it. I remembered my Aunt Pauline trying it once when I was younger. It hadn't gone so well. Gamma ended up hitting her with a frying pan.

"Good," she moaned. "Whinny! Come in here and see what the cat dragged in!" She smiled at me, almost evilly.

Gamma had always been around and living in the house, though Grandma Whinny had run the household for as long as I could remember. Gamma, great-grandma Deloris, had thirteen kids. I think she'd had her first one when she was just fourteen. Ten of them were dead, and all of them had left home in their younger years. The girls married and moved in with their husbands and of the three boys, two died while in war, and one died in a house fire when I was thirteen. Grandma Whinny and Grandpa Bobby had apparently moved back into the house after falling on hard times, many, many years ago and for whatever reason, they never left.

I wasn't sure how Grandma Whinny came to be in charge, but she was, and Gamma never seemed to mind.

Gamma was as mean as a rattlesnake.

Wicked most would say.

I'd even heard stories when I was younger about her dabbling in things like voodoo and witchcraft; of course, there was never any proof. Though I didn't find it hard to believe. To me, she somewhat looked like a witch.

Dark beady eyes and a long, pointed nose.

She was always fussing and cursing about something and most of the time, we, the children, tried to stay the hell out of her way. She thought that spanking was the answer to everything and she didn't mind slapping you with her backhand over the slightest thing.

She was stern, country and hardly ever used proper English, but she was a wise old bat, and she'd seen and experienced things that I couldn't imagine going through.

She had no problem sharing how hard things used to be for her and our family as a child, but she appreciated it for what it was; though if you asked me, she was about sixty plus years overdue for therapy.

I've never heard her say the words *I love you*.

To anyone.

Ever.

I've never heard Grandma Whinny say the words either.

I wasn't sure if it was how they were raised, or maybe showing emotions and love during such hard times was a sign of weakness when they were growing up, but they never told us that they loved us. We knew that they did. They showed us that they cared, but those three words, in the same sentence, at the same time, never escaped from their lips.

It just simply wasn't a part of their vocabulary.

And it had hardly been a part of my mama's.

Sometimes, it was as though she forced herself to say the words to me. It was as though she wasn't sure what they actually meant or if she deserved to say them at all.

I stared at Gamma.

Her long gray hair rested on her shoulders, right on top of the floral nightgown that she was wearing, although it was late into the day. Her brown skin was wrinkled in every direction, yet it glistened as though she'd bathed in coconut oil. She wasn't the plus-sized woman that she'd used to be. Now, she was thin and even uglier than she'd been before.

"It's nice to see you Gamma," I forced myself to say.

"Um huh," she responded and then she yelled again. "Whinny!"

"Damn it, Ma! What in the hell do you want!" I heard grandma's distinctive voice.

Nerves stirred around in my belly.

I was worried about her reaction.

Grandma Whinny was a force to be reckoned with.

She was no joke.

She wasn't as mean and sadistic as Gamma, but she was the one that no one ever wanted to have to deal with. She was as tough as nails. As strong as an ox. As dominant and demanding as a queen on a throne and she didn't take any shit...from anybody!

And I was sure that she was going to have a few choice words from me.

"Ma, what is it? I told you I was---"

Grandma stopped dead in her tracks once she saw me. She stared at me for a while and then finally, she spoke.

"Vana is that you?"

Vana is the nickname that she used to call me.

"Hi grandma," I mumbled. For some reason, I felt like I wanted to cry. Maybe I missed her more than I thought I had. Or perhaps I was afraid, though I wasn't exactly sure why.

Grandma smiled at me, and then suddenly she frowned.

"I ought to slap the piss out of you! You ain't came 'round here and how many years? I taught you betta' than that! You don't walk out on family, girl!"

Well.

She's still the same!

I let her indulge in her little rant, without saying a word and I didn't move until she asked me to.

"Now, come here and give yo' granny a hug," she reached out her arms. She was smiling, but I could still see the disappointment in her eyes.

I rushed into her arms and nestled my head into her bosom.

I sniffed her.

She smelled like *Bengay*, baby powder, and bacon all combined into one. *Grandma.*

She hugged me for a while and then she pulled away from me. She grabbed me by the shoulders and looked me directly in the eyes. "Okay, so what *done* sent you this way, huh?"

She released me and then she put her hands on her hips.

"Folks only come back 'round here for one or two reasons. Either they're runnin' from somethin'. Or lookin' for somethin'. Which reason brought you?"

I didn't know what to say, so I said nothing.

"She looks just like her daddy," Gamma mumbled.

I looked at her.

My daddy?

I don't even know who my daddy is.

I've never met him.

Mama always said that he loved me, but that he had to get himself together before he could come and see me. That was the lie that she told me when I was younger. Once I was older, I knew that what she really meant was that he didn't want to have anything to do with me.

"Oh Ma, just hush! And mind yo' own business! Stop bringin' up stuff to stir up trouble!" Grandma Whinny blurted out.

"Who da' hell you talkin' to? I'm *yo'* mama! And this is *my* mouth! I can say whateva' I damn well please," Gamma rolled her eyes and then turned her attention back to the T.V. She was watching what we called the stories. I hadn't watched the stories in years. I found it funny that they had the small flat screen T.V. sitting on top of the old floor model T.V. that they'd had since I was a little girl.

Grandma didn't reply to her. Instead, she spoke to me. "Whoo chile, you still skinny, I see. New Yorkers must not make good food like we do, huh?"

"No. They don't," I answered grandma truthfully. I'd never come across soul food like I'd grown up eating here. It never had the right amount of seasoning. It never tasted just right. It never *tasted* like home.

Grandma Whinny was big boned, short, and dark like black coffee. She looked almost identical to Gamma, except for her nose. She had a fat, flat, pig nose and it took up too much space on her face.

Oh, but she talked just as bad as Gamma did. I used to talk that way. Improper English and with a thick southern accent, but that had changed over the years. I'd had to work on my speaking for a while to blend in. Now, coming from being an editor and all, I was always correcting a person's grammar inside my head.

In the south, sometimes, they forgot to add the letter 'g' to the end of the words, and it was almost as though words were stopped short. I called it lazy talking. Instead of saying 'your', often they said 'yo'. And so on, and so forth. Hopefully, I don't pick up old habits from being around and talking to them.

Grandma Whinny always wore bright, colorful scarves on her head, even though she had a head full of the thickest, most beautiful hair that I'd ever seen. She was wearing a blue jean dress, but the scarf on her head was a bright yellow. I smiled once I noticed that she was barefoot.

She'd always hated to wear shoes.

"Come on," she said to me and turned around for me to follow her through the house.

It was a lot.

Seeing the family photos all over the walls, the familiar smells and the rooms that hadn't changed or been updated since the day I left.

It was all…a lot.

I felt as though I'd just stepped out of a time machine.

I was dazed. I was overwhelmed. Still, I followed her through the kitchen and out the back door onto the porch.

Still barefoot, grandma sat down in a chair in front of two pots. She was peeling potatoes.

"So…are you goin' to tell me what's goin' on witcha' shug?"

Shug.

I haven't heard that word in such a long time.

Grandma allowed the peelings to drop into the small pot. And then as she cut, she let those pieces fall into the larger pot.

"I just needed to get away," I cleared my throat.

"And come here? After all this time? Sounds like bullshit to me."

I could feel her looking at me, but I kept my eyes on the potatoes.

"You ran away from here, from us, like life was so bad."

It was.

"And now here you are. At the same house that you were born in. On the same porch you played on. And you barely *got* two words to say."

Barely got?

Her talking was going to drive me crazy!

I took a deep breath. I knew that she wasn't going to lay off until I said something that she wanted to hear.

"I'm writing a book."

"A book? A book about what?"

I shrugged. "I don't know yet. Hopefully being here will help me figure it out."

She made a few random noises before she spoke again. "And yo' husband is okay wit' that? With you bein' here?"

Of course, I hadn't told them about the divorce.

None of them had ever met Nathaniel.

I didn't even invite them to the wedding.

They'd found out about my marriage from seeing pictures of us on our wedding day all over social media. Once I finally answered their phone calls, grandma ripped me a new asshole. She called me everything but a child of God for not telling them that I was getting married. And of course, she'd had plenty to say about *who* I'd married and about him not being the color that she would've wanted him to be.

"Yes. Nathaniel is fine with it," I lied.

"Are y'all doin' okay?"

"Yes. We're fine."

"Umph. Then where is yo' ring?" She questioned.

Damn it!

"How long?"

"How long what?"

"How long have you been divorced?"

I exhaled. "What? How…"

"How did I know? 'Cause I'm not stupid, chile," grandma looked insulted.

I exhaled. "It's been finalized for months. Nathaniel left me about a year ago though," finally, I admitted to her.

Grandma sucked her teeth. "What did he do?"

"It was me. It's what I didn't do. It's complicated."

"I bet it is."

"Look, I don't want to be judged…"

"Girl, ain't nobody judging you. I was married to yo' granddaddy for what---48 years? And he cheated on me for 43 of them. At least from what I know of."

What?

Surprisingly, she giggled.

"No judge and jury here. I chose to stay. You chose to leave. Now, we're both free."

I was still trying to wrap my head around the fact that grandpa Bobby had cheated on her. They got along so well when I was growing up. They were the complete opposites from one another yet somehow, they made the perfect fit. Now, they'd always slept in separate bedrooms, for as long as I could remember, but that was normal; at least around here it was. Every set of grandparents that I knew growing up slept in different bedrooms after a certain age.

I thought it was normal.

And grandma...she knew that he was cheating on her and she didn't do anything about it? She'd stayed with him?

I couldn't believe it!

Not Mrs. Whinny FloMae Lynch!

After all the talks she'd given me while I was growing up on how a man was supposed to treat me. Never in a million years would I think that she would accept grandpa cheating on her.

"I'm old school, and divorce wasn't an option for me. Death was his only way out. And finally, he died. Thank God because I was sick of him." She grinned again as she reached for another potato. "Yes indeed, I'd been waitin' on him to go on home to glory for years. I'd been waitin' for my peace of mind for a long time. And I finally got it. Chile, I couldn't get him in the ground fast enough. And his little whore wasn't invited to the funeral either...with her ugly self."

"Wait, so you know her? You knew who she was the whole time?"

"Of course, I knew. And I knew about the kids too."

"Kids!"

"Grown ass men now, but yes, kids. He had two boys with her, and they look just like his raggedy ass too. God rest his soul," she hissed.

Grandma and grandpa also only had two kids.

Mama and Uncle Willie.

Uncle Willie dealt with mental issues. He'd been diagnosed with Schizophrenia when he was about twenty-one. Grandma was also convinced that Uncle Willie had some type of personality disorder as well. Some days, he was 'normal'. And other days, he would raise pure hell. Sometimes he hallucinated and had delusions and then there were days that he appeared to be someone else. That's why grandma thought that the doctors had missed something. His medicine always got him back on track though. His behavior scared the other kids, but not me. As strange as it may sound, once he got into one of his moods, I would sit close by just to watch him. Just to study him. I always wanted to know what it was that flipped his switch, though I could never quite figure it out.

And grandpa was always so kind and patient with him. He loved his son, and even when Uncle Willie was having one of his bad days, grandpa was always right there. It was weird though. Though grandpa Bobby always had his back, Uncle Willie somehow seemed to be more attached to grandma; which I never understood. All she ever seemed to do was curse and fuss at him.

Still, hearing the truth about grandpa was shocking. He'd always been so quiet and humble. So calm and relaxed. Such a family man. I never would've guessed it. And he'd had two kids with his mistress?

Grandma, how dumb can you be for staying with him after that?

I wouldn't dare ask her that question.

"I got the last laugh. She, his mistress, came to ask me if she and the boys could be at the service. You know, that was the only time she ever spoke to me. We'd known about each other for many, many years. We'd crossed paths so many times, but she never said a word to me. Never offered an apology. Never bothered to send my cheating ass husband home. Never decided to go out and find a husband of her own. Never did any of that. But the day after Bobby died, she came right on over here and asked me if she could be there. If his sons could be there. If they could say goodbye. And I looked that devil right in her face and with great pleasure and a satisfied soul I said…hell no."

The way that she'd said it almost made me snicker, but I knew better than to laugh because it was no laughing matter. So, I swallowed my laughter and continued to listen.

"I smiled so big, Vana. And I didn't feel bad about it either. I sure didn't. All those years of layin' on her back, openin' up her legs to a married man, and in the end, she couldn't even see him be put into the ground. I'd lived through years of shame and embarrassment, but she was left with nothin'. He left everything to me. Can't be sure which of us was the dumbest throughout the years, but it sure did feel good to finally win."

If that's what she wanted to call it.

Grandma exhaled, and I could tell that she was relieved. It was as though she'd never told anyone grandpa's terrible secret.

And of all people, she told me.

"You know that you are welcome to stay here. As long as you need to. Yo' old room is still back there. In fact, no one has slept in it since you left."

"No one has slept in that room in fifteen years?"

"Nope. I go in there, clean it and change the sheets, every now and then, but when folks stay over, they never stay back there."

The plantation house had eight old bedrooms and three bathrooms.

My bedroom had been one of three on the bottom floor. I liked it because it had been painted pink, long before I was born, and it had white butterflies all over the walls. It was far at the back of the house, which as a teenager, I'd loved. I would sneak out the window or sneak my boyfriend into it once everyone in the house was asleep.

"So, tell me somethin' Vana. Tell me the truth. Why did you really leave?" Grandma asked.

I turned to face her, but I didn't reply.

I would never tell her or anyone else why.

~***~

My nose led me to the kitchen.

I couldn't remember the last time I'd smelled so many mouthwatering things, all at once.

I entered the kitchen to see that bowls of grits, eggs, bacon, livermush; which is what we called it instead of calling it liver pudding. Biscuits and molasses and pancakes were all on the table. And grandma was at the stove frying pork chops.

"Mawnin' Vana."

"Good morning."

"How did you sleep?"

I didn't.

Being back in my old room made me more emotional than a Cancer attending a wedding and a funeral on the same day. Cancers, from the zodiac signs, were always so damn sensitive. And last night, so was I.

I cried all night long as I relived pain and memories. And as I thought about Mama.

My mother, Glorianne Lynch, was murdered my senior year of high school.

I'd won homecoming queen the night before, and I was on the high of my life. All I could think about was that prom would be coming soon and I wanted to be crowned queen then too. That's all that was on my mind. Well, graduation and college were also on my mind at the time. Up until then, life hadn't been perfect, but it had been okay. It had been normal. And then it all changed. That next day, I noticed that mama hadn't come home the night before. I was mad at her. I was mad because she wasn't there and because she broke her promise. I didn't know that she didn't come home because she was dead.

Mama was found dead in a cotton field with her work clothes still on. She'd suffered a single, fatal blow to the side of her head.

She was murdered. Someone killed her.

The police were sure that she was killed somewhere else and then moved to the field; especially since her car had been found miles away from the crime scene.

No one had seen anything.

No one could think of anyone who would've wanted to kill her, and the police didn't have much to go on.

The murder weapon was never found. Mama hadn't been sexually violated. She'd been at work for hours the day before, so she'd had all kinds of DNA all over her; including animals and mine. There weren't any cameras around the abandoned building where her car was found. The door of her car was left wide open, and her purse was still inside. She hadn't been seen at the bar that night, but according to the reports, she had a good bit of alcohol in her system when she died. There was an empty bottle of liquor found in her car. She'd been spotted earlier that night, right after work, but apparently, they couldn't find anything or anyone that had seen her closer to the time of her death. The area where she was found was out of city limits. Had it not been harvest season, there's no telling when they would've found her. They didn't find anything suspicious at the scene. All they found was her. As if she'd just been dumped there.

For a long time, I waited for something to happen. For someone to come forward, but no one ever did.

Her murder shook the small town, and it made it almost impossible for me to go anywhere without someone reminding me that I'd lost her. Then came all the rumors, and I found myself constantly defending my mother's name.

It was horrible.

It didn't take long for the police to give up on her case. Honestly, I don't think they really cared. They didn't seem to be too worried about catching her killer, but even when they stopped looking---I didn't.

I would catch the bus and then walk the rest of the way to the field, almost every day, just to walk around. Hoping to find something. Hoping to see something that the police missed. Something that would bring my mother justice and bring me some kind of peace.

I never found anything, and that day of justice never came.

"Sit down and eat somethin'," Gamma growled.

I took a seat.

When mama died, for the first time ever, I wished that I hadn't been an only child. It would've been nice to have a sibling to go through it with me. Someone that I could talk to that would understand.

I was Grandma Whinny's *only* grandchild, but she had tons of great nieces and nephews that for some reason called her grandma too. I'm not sure why or who started it, but grandma never corrected them.

To sum it up, Gamma, my great-grandma Deloris had thirty-six great-grandchildren, including me, and most of them spent plenty of time at the plantation house with me while I was growing up.

My cousin Marlo and I had always been pretty close. She was three years older than I was and my great-aunt Bertha Mae's granddaughter; so technically, she was like my second cousin, but we never worried about all of that. I'd also had a pretty close bond with my cousins Eve, Tatiana and Roxanne too. And a love-hate relationship with my cousin Cassy. There were plenty of other female cousins that were either a lot older or a lot younger than I was. So, I wasn't around them too much back then. And we had a host of male cousins too.

Still, none of them were my siblings, and they had no idea what it was like to be me. They just couldn't understand what I was going through.

"This is a lot of food."

"Trust me, it's gonna' get eaten," grandma said, just as voices called out her name.

"Grandma Whinny? Gamma?"

I heard what sounded like a herd of people and then seconds later the kitchen was flooded with people that I hadn't seen in years. And some little people that I've never met before.

Family.

All of them were my family.

I couldn't help but wonder how many great-great-grandchildren Gamma had. I refused to try to count the heads of the ones in the room.

As soon as they noticed me, they went crazy!

Hugs and kisses came from every direction and the questions. There were so many questions.

"How old are you now?"

"Thir---let's just say thirty-something," I laughed.

"How long are you in town?"

"I don't know."

"Look at your lips. Have you had work done?"

"No."

And the questions continued for quite a while.

"What is New York like? Is it different from here?"

"Very."

"I would love to visit, but I've never been invited," my cousin Eve said, sarcastically.

Eve, Cassy, and Roxanne were sisters and my great-Aunt Pauline's granddaughters. Their mother left them on Aunt Pauline years ago when we were younger. She just dropped them off to her one day and told her to her face that she wasn't coming back to get them. No one knew where she was; at least not back then. I wasn't sure if they had seen her since I've been away. I wondered if they would even want to. Aunt Pauline took them in and raised them as best as she could. And what she couldn't do, Grandma Whinny picked up the slack. Aunt Pauline was grandma's sister. She was the oldest of the girls, and she was one of the three children of Gamma's that were still alive.

My cousins Tatiana and Marlo were siblings. Their grandma was my great Aunt Bertha Mae, who was also still alive but not doing so well these days, according to grandma. Their mother was still alive, but she and Grandma Whinny had a disagreement back in 1985, and to this very day, neither of them wanted to apologize to the other. They were both still holding a grudge, so their mother, Hazel, never came around. I've never ever seen her come to the plantation house. The only time I would see her was at a wedding or a funeral. And she and grandma never spoke to each other in those settings either. As far as I knew, and since she wasn't here, they were probably still on the outs. And it's been over 30 years. Talk about holding a grudge!

The good thing about it all is that she never stopped her girls from coming to the house and grandma never treated them any different from the rest of us. Hell, Marlo had practically lived there with us for most of my childhood.

"I've missed you," Roxanne said, but my cousin Cassy rolled her eyes.

"I don't know why y'all actin' like she's some kind of celebrity or something. She's the same ole' Savannah. Ain't nothing changed about her.

Y'all act like she deserves a cookie or something for comin' home. She's the one that left. She's the one that cut us off and got all brand new. She didn't want to be a part of this family then, so why the hell is she here trying to be a part of it now?"

"Chile, you betta' shut yo' damn mouth before I put my fist in it! And I mean you shut it right now! Just go on and hush up, now!" Grandma hissed at her just as she placed a plate full of pork chops on the table. "Family is family. She's here now. Don't make *no* difference why."

I corrected grandma's grammar in my head.

Everyone, except for Cassy, nodded in agreeance.

"I'm just saying. She could've at least said goodbye," Cassy complained.

"Cass, I didn't even know that I was leaving. I just got the idea and decided to go. I didn't tell anyone goodbye. And then once I was gone...I just didn't want to come back." I said to her. She didn't say anything.

"Word on the street is that some New York City chick is in the house," I heard suddenly from behind me.

Marlo.

She reached her baby to a cousin nearby, and she rushed towards me and hugged my neck.

"Hey cousin," she smiled at me.

I hugged her back. "Hey."

Marlo had kept up with me here and there over the years. We would chat on social media, and sometimes we would speak over the phone. She was married with a house full of kids, just like everyone else around here, but whenever I crossed her mind, she didn't mind reaching out and letting me know. Sometimes I would answer her calls. And sometimes, I wouldn't.

"I can't believe that you're here! And that you didn't tell me you were coming!"

"I didn't know that I was coming until I got here," I admitted to her.

"Mama is she white?" Her daughter asked her. I remembered seeing her pictures on Marlo's social media pages.

I'd straightened my curly hair the night before and wondered if that was why she was confused.

"Yes," Gamma scuffed with a chuckle.

"No baby, she's not white. She's just light-skinned."

Her daughter didn't seem convinced. She pointed out that her baby brother was light-skinned and that I was lighter than he was. The room fell quiet and awkward for a while, and then someone changed the subject.

"Why didn't you bring your husband? Do you have kids?"

"No husband and no kids."

I could see Gamma staring at me in confusion.

"I've been divorced for a few months, and we never had kids. It was never the right time."

"What? So, in that big city, you have to schedule a time to fuc---"

"Gamma!"

Every adult in the room yelled at the same time.

"What?" She growled.

"With my job and his job, we just never got around to it. Now that we aren't together, I guess it's a good thing."

"Umph, if you say so," Gamma mumbled.

"So, shall we eat?" Grandma tried to move the conversation along. "Kids you know where to go. Eve and Marlo, help me fix their plates."

The kitchen got busy for a while, but finally, the kids were settled in another room, and all of the adults in the house were seated at the long kitchen table; except for Uncle Willie.

Grandma disappeared to take a plate to his bedroom. Since none of my male cousins or any of the husbands were there, I figured that grandma had only called around to invite the women and children. She must've called them and told them I was here.

"How long are you staying?" Marlo questioned.

"We already asked this question," Cassy barked.

"I don't know," I answered Marlo anyway. "I'm writing a book and---"

"A book?"

"Yes."

"About us?" Cassy questioned.

"I have no idea what the book is going to be about. I haven't started it yet. I've tried to write it a few times, but nothing came to me. So, I decided to get away from the city for a while and find some inspiration. I ended up here."

"In Clover? You went looking for inspiration and ended up in Clover, South Carolina?" Tatiana questioned.

I simply nodded.

I tried not to stare at her.

She looked so different.

She was probably one of the prettiest women that'd ever seen. And I'd seen so many different types of women in the city.

Tatiana looked like a real-life, black Barbie doll. And I couldn't find a single thing wrong with her. She didn't have a single flaw. Her skin was as dark as burnt rubber, but it was even and smooth. And her makeup was flawless. Her makeup really brought out her light brown eyes and luscious lips. She wore her hair in a high ponytail, and it was full of natural curls. She had on gold hoop earrings, with matching bangles, a crop top underneath a black jacket that was undone and ripped jeans. Her stomach was flat, but her hips and thighs were proof that she'd been eating cornbread and ham hocks all her life. Tatianna had grown into her big forehead, and she had fixed her teeth. And from the size of the rock on her hand, I was sure that she had snagged someone who was probably just obsessed with her beauty as I was.

"Yeah, I'm surprised that I ended up here, but here I am," I stuttered.

"Chile, if you were looking for inspiration, you should've ended up in Hawaii or something," Roxanne giggled. "Nothing is inspiring about this town. Not one darn thing."

Grandma came back into the kitchen and sat to the right of me. She touched my shoulder, and once she got comfortable, we said grace and then the conversation was turned up a few notches.

Grandma still had a way of livening up the room. We reminisced, laughed and shared a few stories. I remembered the things that I actually liked about having a big family. If only the good had outweighed the bad fifteen years ago, maybe I wouldn't have left.

"So, I know everyone wants to know...how was that ex-husband of yours in the sack?" Eve asked, causing an outburst of laughter from most of the women in the room.

"Eve," grandma glared at her.

"What? We all want to know. At least I do. I've never been with a white man before."

I shrugged. "Actually, Nathaniel is the best I've ever had. As a matter of fact, no one has ever compared. They haven't even come close."

"Ooh really? Not even Jace?"

Jace.

I was trying not to think about Jace.

"Jace and I were young."

"Young...but you loved the hell out of that damn boy," Marlo said as she took a bite out of her pork chop. "And Cassy did too."

What did she just say?

"Don't be messy, Marlo," Grandma Whinny chimed in.

"What? I'm not. I'm just saying. Once you were gone Savannah, Cassy tried to shoot her shot. She tried to get with Jace. He was fair game."

I could see that Cassy was uncomfortable, but she tried to laugh it off.

Cassy wanted to be with Jace?

My first love? My first everything?

Yeah. Now I remember why I never really liked her.

"Yeah, I guess I wasn't light enough for him. Maybe he has something against dark-skinned chicks," Cassy said. She was dark-skinned, but she had a cute face. It was her attitude that had always made her ugly.

"Or maybe it just had something to do with the fact that you're my cousin," I snarled at her.

"Touché," she shrugged. "I didn't really want him. He was just nice to look at. That's all. It wasn't like y'all were married or anything. Shit, anyone I was with before the age of twenty-one...they don't count. I was young. I didn't know what I wanted before then. I was horny and retarded," Cassy giggled.

Everyone laughed, except for me.

Why was I angry?

"Seriously, it wasn't like that," Cassy said.

"So, the sex was good, and from that car outside and the pictures I've seen online, the money was good too...so why the divorce?" Tatiana brought the conversation back to my ex-husband Nathaniel.

I pushed my plate away.

"Sometimes things just don't work out."

"They can if you want them to."

I looked around at the table.

It was seven other women outside of grandma, Gamma and me; including two other cousins that didn't come around as much when we were younger. All of them were proclaiming to be happily married.

I'd been happy with Nathaniel.

And before I reneged on giving him kids, I was sure that he'd been happy with me too. I never caught him in any lies and as far as I knew he had never cheated on me.

The divorce was all because of me.

When he left me, at first, I kept trying to get him back. I tried everything except for the obvious. Except for what he wanted. I still refused to get pregnant, and he made it clear that he wasn't going to change his mind about kids. So, I called his bluff. I thought he wasn't going to do it. I was sure that he wouldn't go through with the divorce.

I was wrong.

I was dead wrong.

He left me, divorced me, and moved on.

And it was all my fault.

Thankfully, the conversation shifted from being all about me, and we conversed for another hour or so, about everything from love to politics.

It was a Saturday, and everyone made plans to stay at the house all day. Most of them checked in with their husbands and decided to stay overnight. It was going to be a house full all day and night, and everybody seemed to be excited about it.

Grandma and Gamma agreed to look after the kids for a couple of hours, so five of us ladies decided to take a drive downtown.

Now, downtown Clover was nothing like I'd grown accustomed to. It was merely made up of a few brick buildings, small shops, and stores. And a few restaurants, but nothing spectacular. It was nothing like downtown Manhattan.

Marlo was celebrating her tenth-year marriage anniversary, and they were having a party. She was having her dress tailored by one of the shops, so that was our first stop.

I'll admit, though I was usually comfortable in social settings and had tons of friends back in New York, with my cousins, around them, I felt slightly out of place.

As though I didn't belong.

Just like I used to feel when I was younger.

"Wow, you look amazing!" Eve squealed at the sight of Marlo standing in front of us in her dress. We all nodded in agreeance.

"It isn't too much, is it?"

"No. It's perfect," I assured Marlo just as my phone started to ring.

I glanced down at it to see that it was Nathaniel.

The divorce has been final for months. Nathaniel and I are now in a better place. During the divorce, he'd acted as though he was more hurt than I was. He fought, tugged, and pulled for things to go his way. He barely got the results he wanted though. I got to keep my car, the house and some of his money.

Nathaniel was a hotshot plastic surgeon, but strangely, he adored natural beauty. With no makeup on and on my worst day, he would act as though I was the prettiest girl in the world. And I better not so much as mention having any work done. He would have a fit! He loved me just as I was. He never went a day without complimenting me. All he ever wanted was to love me and get me pregnant.

And I pushed him away. And now, he was having a baby with someone else. She was giving him the one thing that he's always wanted, and in return, I was pretty sure that he was going to suck it up and give her the world.

My world. At least it was supposed to be.

"Excuse me," I said to everyone, and I headed out of the shop to take his call.

"Hello?"

"I've been calling you for the past few days," he said immediately.

"What is it, Nathaniel?"

I didn't care that Nathaniel was white. To me, he was one of the sexiest men on God's green earth. He was handsome, and a little edgy. He'd grown up in the Bronx, so he knew all about soul food, Hip Hop and he had plenty of African American friends. As folks often said, he had a little *swag* to him.

"I have something that I want to talk to you about."

"Like what? Shouldn't you be with your baby's mama? Or something?"

I wasn't sure why I was acting nasty towards him. Usually, I would be sitting around hoping that he decided to call or text me.

"I didn't call to argue with you Savannah. Where are you? Can you meet me somewhere?"

"I can't. I'm out of town."

"Where?"

"None of your business. You divorced me, remember?"

Nathaniel said a few more things, and then he told me that he had to go. I hung up, wishing that I hadn't acted like an asshole. We didn't have any bad blood between us. Once we'd signed on the dotted line, Nathaniel had gone back to acting like himself again. The sweet and calm man that I'd always known him to be.

We agreed to always remain friends. I guess I was just on edge.

Being here made me that way.

I turned around to walk back into the shop.

"Oops, sorry!" I touched the arm of the man that I had just bumped into.

"Don't worry about it. It's okay," the man smiled at me.

I smiled back at him.

"You're not from around here, are you?" He asked.

"Actually, I am. Born and raised."

"Really? I've never seen anyone as pretty as you around here before. What side of town?"

He didn't look like someone I would've known from back then either.

He was gorgeous.

He had a beard, with a bald head.

Tall, muscular, and...*vanilla*.

"I'm pretty sure we're from different sides," I giggled.

"Smart ass," he laughed. "I like it. I'm Kori. Sheriff Kori," he said reaching out his hand.

"I'm Savannah. Just Savannah," I shook his hand.

"Savannah. I like that name. Maybe I'll bump into you again sometime. Or maybe we can bump into each other on purpose next time," he said, reaching me a card.

"Maybe."

He eyed me flirtatiously as I reached for the handle on the shop's door.

"Nice meeting you Savannah."

"Likewise."

Back inside, the girls were chatting, and after promising Marlo that I would stay in town for at least another week to attend her anniversary party, after stopping at a few more places, we piled into her oversized SUV and headed back towards the house.

Strangely, everyone was silent on the way there.

I kept glancing at the card in my hand.

Nathaniel is the only man that I have been with, sexually, in almost eight years.

I hadn't thought much about dating, but maybe it would be a good thing. I had no plans on staying here, but since I was staying for at least another week, maybe I could get out and use Mr. Kori as practice; or sex. Either way, I had to get comfortable with putting myself back out there again.

Back at the house, we walked in a line up the crooked steps. We could hear the kids yelling and screaming before we even opened the door.

It reminded me of back in the day.

Grandma Whinny, Gamma and some of the other grown folks that had stayed behind were all seated in the living room. The rest of us joined them by taking a seat anywhere that we could. I sat on the floor next to grandma's legs.

"Everything ready?" She asked Marlo.

"Yes. The dress is perfect. Oh, I was going to ask you if the kids could stay here with you for the five days that we'll be going away. We were going to ask Luis's parents, but there's no sense in them having to drive from Rock Hill every morning to take Noel and Aaliyah to school if they can stay here with you. Pleassssse," she begged.

Grandma fussed at her about being unorganized, but she said yes. "What's that?" Grandma asked me, as I twirled the card around between my index finger and thumb. Before I could answer her, she snatched the card from my grasp.

"I bumped into a police officer at the shop. Well, he said that he was the Sheriff. He basically asked me out on a date and gave me his card," I confessed. The ladies in the room either giggled or started to chatter.

"Kori?"

"Yeah, that was his name. You know him?"

"Hmm…The only Sheriff Kori I know…" grandma started, but Gamma interrupted her and finished her sentence.

"Is yo' damn brother!"

Huh?

My brother? What brother?

****

CHAPTER TWO

I think that's him.

Grandma told me where I could find the man that was supposed to be my daddy.

Hesitantly, after Gamma's outburst the other day, Grandma Whinny hadn't had a choice but to tell me my mother's secret.

She told me the truth.

And the truth was...my daddy is a white man.

A married white man at that.

He owned one of the local hardware stores. The most popular one in town. I remembered going by there with mama, at least a dozen times that I could recall. I always stayed in the car while she went inside. She always told me that she was just running in to get something and that she would be right back. Thinking back, she never came out of the store with anything in her hand. Not even once.

She was going to see him.

She had to be.

Why didn't he ask to see me?

I couldn't believe that grandma had known who my father was all this time. However, all she said was that it hadn't been her secret to share. Grandma said that she thought the truth had died with mama, but thanks to Gamma's big mouth the truth was out.

"Excuse me, ma'am, can I help you?"

I stared at him.

I didn't know what to say.

As a young girl, I always thought about my father.

I always thought about what I would say to him if I ever got to meet him. I would imagine what he looked like, but the man standing in front of me was nothing like I'd imagined my daddy to be.

He was an older man, gray, and his teeth were so white and straight that they had to be dentures. He was overly dressed and wore an expensive watch. You could tell that he was the owner of the store. I wondered why he was there in the first place. I'd counted at least three employees walking around. The man looked as though he could've been relatively handsome back in the day. And maybe, kind of, in some ways, he looked like...me.

Sheriff Kori didn't look anything like him at all.

"Can I help you?"

I shook my head. "No."

I walked out of the store in a hurry. I held my breath until I was inside of my car with the doors locked.

Why wouldn't she tell me?

Once I was old enough to understand, mama should've told me the truth. Whether he was married or not, I'd had a right to know. I'd had the right to know who my daddy was.

I've always known that there had to be a reason why she wouldn't tell me much about him. If I had to guess, he probably didn't know that I was his. Or maybe he did.

Maybe he knew about me and just didn't care.

Maybe he never wanted to know me.

Maybe mama lied to me to protect me from the truth.

Maybe that was the only way to keep me from feeling unwanted and rejected.

Then why was she always coming here to see him?

45

If he hadn't wanted anything to do with me, then surely, she wouldn't want anything to do with him.

Right?

You see.

This is why I've always avoided coming back here. This feeling. This exact feeling. This is how I felt on the day that I'd ran away.

Confused. Broken. Emotional and unfulfilled.

I never should've come back!

I started up my car just as I spotted Sheriff Kori walking into the hardware store.

I assumed that he was heading inside to see *our* father.

Jealousy forced its way into my heart just as I drove away.

What about me?

I drove circles around the small town for what seemed like forever until finally, I ended up in front of a coffee shop.

For a while, I sat there with my fingers tapping against the steering wheel. I thought about going back to the hardware store, but the fear of rejection wouldn't let me. Instead, I grabbed my purse and my laptop and scurried into the coffee shop.

After ordering two cups of coffee, at the same time, I found an empty table, and once I was settled, I opened my laptop. I opened it to a blank page, and I placed my fingers over the keys on the keyboard. I closed my eyes. And then...

I started to type.

Untitled.

If I told you the story of my life, I'm not sure you would believe me.

My first sentence.

I wrote my very first sentence, and I didn't stop there.

Words started to pour out of my heart and onto the pages so fast that my fingers could barely keep up. My words were emotional and transparent. Heartfelt and full of rage and pain. Racing against time to type my next word, I became so consumed with my thoughts and absorbed with my emotions, that I felt as though I was no longer in control of my body. I couldn't stop my fingers from typing. I couldn't stop *telling* my story. And honestly, I didn't want to.

For the first time, writing my book was effortless. Writing was therapy; a session that felt as though it could've gone on and on forever. It was so therapeutic, for me, to be able to take my feelings and regrets and give them to someone else; some make-believe person in my story that in the end and unlike in the real world, I had the final say. I controlled the outcome. I wasn't sure of how long I had been there, writing, and I didn't have any plans to stop until… I looked up. On the other side of the coffee shop's window, right in front of me, I saw a woman. A woman who used to be a girl, that I used to love and know. A girl who used to be my best friend.

Livy.

Livy and I had grown up around each other just like most of us had. We went to the same schools. The same church and we sang in the same choir. She was an only child just like I was, so naturally, we attached ourselves to one another and spent a lot of time together.

She was my first friend. My closest friend. My entire childhood. And I thought that nothing would ever tear us apart.

I was wrong.

Something did.

"Livy?" I asked as soon as I walked out of the coffee shop. I heard the old door slam shut behind me. I was holding my purse in one hand and my laptop close to my chest, staring at the back of the woman, waiting for her to answer me.

"Livy?"

"Yeah, who wants to know?" She said before turning around to face me.

Wait...

Is she...is she..high?

Yes.

Yes, she is.

I couldn't be sure of what she was *on,* but she was on something. By instinct, I inspected her. She had on shoes and clean clothes, so someone had to be caring for her. She didn't look homeless, but as I continued to examine her, I noticed that her arms were painted with marks from her poison of choice.

Oh no. Livy.

"Livy?" I repeated her name.

She scrunched up her face, and I could tell that she was trying to think. I could tell that she was trying to remember.

She was trying to remember me.

And then it was as though a lightbulb went off inside her head and her bottom lip started to quiver.

"Savannah? Vana is that you? Is it really you?" She asked.

Just like everyone else, I'd cut her off when I left town. I never spoke to her again. I never reached out to her. I never said goodbye. I did search for her, a few times on social media, just to see her but I never could find her.

"Savannah?" She interrupted my thoughts, yet again asking for confirmation.

"Yes, Livy. It's me. Savannah."

Her eyes filled up with tears.

"Oh my God, it's you. It's really you," she sobbed and walked closer to me. I moved my laptop from my chest and embraced her.

She cried.

Loudly.

She was so loud that people started to stop and stare.

And although I felt something, I didn't shed a tear.

"I can't believe that you're here," Livy blubbered.

"How are you?" I asked her. It sounded like the right thing to say.

Livy pulled away from me.

"A mess, *friend*. For years, I've been one, big mess," she admitted.

"How did this happen to you?"

She shrugged. "Love."

I asked her to walk with me to my car, that way we could talk in private. She approached my car as though it was some type of foreign object.

"Love did what to you?" I asked her once we were both seated inside.

She shook her head as she placed on her seatbelt even though we weren't going anywhere.

"I remember before you left, you wouldn't talk to me anymore. I kept trying to talk to you, but you shut me out. And then one day, I went to your house, and your grandma told me that you weren't there. She didn't have many answers. She just said that you were gone, and that you were never coming back."

Livy couldn't seem to stay still. She moved her fingers, consistently, and her eyes fluttered time and time again. Our little reunion seemed to have brought her down a notch from whatever cloud she'd been on before I approached her.

"Where did you go?"

"Away. I went away. I just had to."

She didn't respond.

"And long story short, I ended up in New York."

"New York?"

"Yes. I've been there for years. I just got back in town the other day. I'm not sure how long I'll be staying. A few years ago, I searched for you a few times online, but…"

"I don't have all of that stuff. I'm sure that you can tell that I haven't been…" She didn't finish her sentence.

"How long have you been like…like this?"

"Too long. It's been a while."

"And someone you loved turned you on to this? Someone you loved did this to you?"

"Isn't that how it goes? Someone you love is usually the one responsible for doing the unthinkable to you. Whether it's physically or mentally. It doesn't really matter. At some point in time…love always hurts."

She started to scratch her arms.

"After you left, I tried to find my way. I didn't know what I wanted to do. I thought that maybe I wanted to leave here too, you know. I tried college for a while. I hated it. It just wasn't for me. Then I thought maybe I could go to school to do hair. We used to love doing each other's hair, remember? I never signed up for the classes though. I found a job instead. And then I met Sajohn. He was older than you and I. About ten years older, so you probably don't remember him. His parents live in that big house on Honeycutt Road."

"Honeycutt Road?" I tried to remember. "Oh, the white and green house?"

"Yeah. That's the one."

"I never knew they had a son."

"He left and went into the army when we would've been about eight years old. Anyway, I met him, and it was the best thing that ever happened to me. He loved me. He moved me in with him. Married me. Gave me everything that I ever wanted. We had a beautiful daughter together. The both of them were my entire world. I was happy. I mean, for once, I was so happy. And then one night, Sajohn was on his way to pick me up from work, and he fell asleep behind the wheel. I lost him that night. I lost both of them. My husband and my daughter both died from the crash. And the passenger of the other car died too. My mama."

Her words stung like a thousand bees.

"Harvey had been driving. He lived. Mama died."

Harvey.

Harvey was Livy's stepfather and...

"Do you know what it's like to lose the best part of you, your entire world, in just one night? My mother, I know that you can relate to that, but my husband and my daughter too? Why would God do that to me? Why would he take my family? He took away everyone that I loved."

The tears poured painfully down her face.

I remember how I felt when mama died. I couldn't imagine the pain that she'd gone through from losing her mother, her husband, and her child all at once.

"Harvey forced her to go out that night. Mama called me while I was at work. She was complaining about Harvey because he'd wanted her to go with him to celebrate one of his friend's promotions and she didn't want to go. But she was going because Harvey told her that everyone else would have their wives there and that he didn't want to go alone. It was always about what Harvey wanted. She was always jumping through hoops for him, just to keep him happy and to keep from hearing him nag and complain. I told her to call me once she got back home because I was working late, and I knew that I would still be awake. Later that night, they were on their way home while Sajohn was on his way to pick me up. What are the odds of them being on the same road, at the exact same time? It's just my bad luck, I guess. My husband caused the head-on collision. One witness said that Sajohn swerved in and out of the lane a few times before the crash. As though he'd been fighting to stay awake. He'd worked all day, then came home to tend to our daughter. I was the one that wanted to pull a double shift. I was the one that wanted all of this extra stuff for our daughter's first birthday, so I was working overtime to get it. All because I'd wanted to impress people that have proven over the years that they don't give a damn about me. Isn't that somethin'? Folks always pretend to care until you actually need them. Sajohn was tired. If only I'd let him pick me up hours before, but I hadn't. And then the witness said that she saw his car heading into the other lane again. She said that she pressed on her horn, but he hadn't heard her. Harvey admitted that he and mama had been arguing and that he didn't see Sajohn's car until it was too late. And then my entire life was destroyed."

Livy opened my car door, but once she noticed that I was in tears, she closed it.

"After that, I just haven't been the same, you know. I just needed somethin' to take away the pain. To get the thoughts out of my head. Alcohol was my go-to for a while, but I started to need somethin' a little stronger. And then I needed somethin' else that was stronger. And stronger."

I leaned over the armrest to hug her. She just sat there.

"I'm tryin' to get myself together. I'm tryin'. I'm really tryin'," she whined.

"It's okay. Everything is going to be okay."

"No, Savannah. It isn't. Everything and everyone that I love is gone." She looked at me. "Would've been nice to have a shoulder to lean on." Livy opened the car door again.

"Wait. Wait. Do you need anything? Money? Food? Rehab? I can help you. Whatever you need, I can help you."

Livy smiled at me.

Her teeth were stained, but they were all still there. Her almond-shaped eyes were bloodshot red from the tears, and she had bags underneath them. In a weird, decayed type of way, she was still beautiful.

"No. I don't need anything. Grandma Whinny makes sure that I have food and a place to go home to. And clean clothes too. I'm okay," she said, and just before she closed the door she said, "Yeah. I'm okay. No thanks to you...*friend*."

And then she let the door slam shut and trotted off.

I watched her until she was out of sight and then I raced home to grandma.

She was looking after Livy.

Why hadn't she told me?

When I arrived at the plantation house, I found grandma in her garden.

"Grandma," I started to sob and then got down on my knees. I hugged her. She hugged me back.

"I saw Livy."

"Oh chile, I wondered when it would be a good time to bring her up. How is she?"

I shook my head.

"I look after her. I have been for a long time. I pay her rent. I keep food in that house and make sure she has clean clothes. I can't make her stop using those drugs, but I can at least do that."

I nodded. "Thank you, grandma, thank you."

She didn't respond.

I told her that I would help her. I told her that I would pay up Livy's rent for a long while and that even once I was gone, I would send money home to cover her food.

"Do you rememba' how to pull weeds, chile?"

It's pronounced 'remember' grandma! Re-mem-ber!

"Yes ma'am," I answered her.

I wiped my eyes with the top of my shirt, and then I moved in front of the tomatoes.

"How long you stayin'?"

"I don't know grandma. Honestly, I want to go home. Like, right now. There are too many memories here. Too much pain."

"Pain is real and most of our reality, girl. Wherever there's pain---there's healing. Nothin' gets healed if you're always runnin'."

I touched one of the tomatoes.

They were almost ripe.

Just in time before the cold weather really started to set in.

For a long while, neither of us said a word. We both worked silently, side by side until we heard shouting up above our heads.

We looked up to see Uncle Willie hanging out of his bedroom window. He was shouting, and out of nowhere, he tossed the house phone out of the window.

"Damn it! Willie!" Grandma yelled as I helped her to her feet. Before we could make it inside, Uncle Willie came out onto the front porch.

"Why the hell did you throw my phone out the window boy?" She questioned him.

He looked at me.

I hadn't spoken to him or seen him since I'd been there. He was always in his bedroom refusing to come out. He'd aged. He looked different. Still tall and brown, but I used to think he and mama looked alike. Looking at him now…they didn't.

He stared at me as though I was a stranger, but to my surprise, he said my name.

"What's up, Savannah."

"What's up my ass! Why did you throw my phone outside?"

"Because."

"Because of what?"

"Because," Uncle Willie started to whisper. "Somebody was listening to my phone call."

"Boy, ain't no damn body listening to yo' phone calls! Who the hell were you on the phone with anyway?"

"Yes, they were. They were trying to catch me. They were on the other end of the phone. Trying to catch me. Trying to see what I was gonna' say."

Grandma huffed. "And who were you on the phone with?"

"Why? Just know that I was on it and somebody was listening to my call. I know what I'm talking about! Don't try to tell me what I'm talking about! I know! I know! They were listening!" Uncle Willie was convinced. Of course, it was probably his mind playing tricks on him again. I couldn't tell whether his condition had gotten worse or if it was still the same. He'd always been paranoid. Delusional. And a lot of other things since I was a child.

"Willie, did you take your medicine today?"

"I ain't taking that medicine!"

"Oh, yes the hell you are!"

"No, I'm not! I'm a grown ass man! I can do whatever I damn well please!"

"Oh, you're a grown ass man, huh? That's what you said right? You gonna' do whatever you damn well please, right?" Grandma threw the phone that she'd picked up at him, and Uncle Willie took off running. She followed right behind, yelling and screaming at him, and all I could do was shake my head.

I guess some things never change.

And then again, some things---some people do.

Oh Livy.

~***~

"How much was that dress? And where did you get it from?" Tatiana asked me.

It was the night of Marlo's anniversary party, and truthfully, I was ready for it to be done and over with. I was ready to go.

The last few days have been quiet.

Normal.

Not much has gone on. I've spent a lot of time with grandma and family. And still, I haven't quite learned all of my little cousins' names.

I've been writing like crazy too. I was already on chapter four of my new book, and it seemed like every day, I had so much more to say. I've found my inspiration and so much more by coming back here. I guess I have to be thankful for that. And now that I have some type of direction and a storyline, I was pretty sure that I could finish writing my book in New York.

I could go back *home*.

"I had my assistant; well, my ex-assistant, overnight it from New York."

She touched my dress, and so did Cassy.

"Well, it's beautiful. Everyone is going to be lookin' at you, instead of the guest of honor," Cassy said, with a tone in her voice that sounded more like an insult instead of a compliment.

"I doubt it. Wait until you see grandma," I assured her, even though my grandma was technically her aunt.

Grandma came up the hallway just in time.

Everyone praised her and complimented her on the $1,000 dress that I'd had sent for her. I'd even gotten her a matching head scarf since she loved to wear them so much.

"Okay, is everybody ready to go?"

We all nodded.

"Gamma, if those kids get up, whoop their asses 'cause I told them to go to bed."

"Shug, you don't have to tell me how to watch kids! I raised thirteen of them! Hell, I raised you. Go on, now. Dance a little for me too," she waved us off and out the door we went.

All of their husbands were waiting for them outside. Marlo and her husband would be arriving at the venue, but as for my other cousins, they all had a handsome, well-dressed man on their arm.

"I guess it's just you and me," grandma smiled.

"I guess so huh?"

We drove about seven minutes away and then we hurried inside of the building to take our seats. Marlo had gone all out for this event. The venue was beautiful. It looked as though she'd spent a fortune on decorations. She'd hired servers, a DJ, a bartender, and her friend, Janice, was the host for the evening.

We sat down for only about a minute before the DJ asked everyone to stand back up and clap for the lovely couple as they made their entrance.

Instantly, the room was filled with applause and roars as they strutted in, hand and hand. They smiled as they made their way to the dance floor, and then they started to dance.

Marlo was glowing, and as I observed the way that she looked at her husband, I couldn't help but think about Nathaniel.

Nathaniel had given me the wedding of my dreams. Anything that I'd wanted he'd made it happen. At first, I'd wanted a church wedding, but then I'd wanted to do something exciting. Something amazing. A day that I would remember for the rest of my life. So, we planned for a wedding in Spain.

Incredible, exhilarating, extraordinary, all of those words were merely understatements to describe my wedding day.

I felt like a princess. I felt so alive.

And then we had our first dance.

On a rooftop, surrounded by candlelight and about fifty of his closest family and our friends. We'd swayed to the soulful sound of Kenny Latimore, bellowing one of my all-time favorite tunes, *For You*, and Nathaniel stared into my eyes as though he'd hit the jackpot. As though he was the luckiest man in the world.

I've never felt so valuable or so wanted. And hopefully someday, I would feel that way again.

I'd been dodging Nathaniel's calls, so I still didn't know what he wanted to talk to me about. I guess it was a blessing and a curse that we didn't hate each other like most divorcees do, but I couldn't help but wonder what was on his mind.

Maybe he was going to tell me that he was going to get remarried to his baby's mother.

I definitely didn't want to hear that.

Though I couldn't say that I would be surprised.

Nathaniel was a good man. And though he hasn't known Nada, the Persian chick, that long, and although they'd gotten pregnant after sleeping together only once, according to what Nathaniel said, I knew that he was probably going to marry her. He would finally have the life, and family that he's always wanted. And quite frankly, it was the life that he deserved.

The sudden clapping brought me back to reality, and once Marlo and Luis took a bow, they headed to take their seats. The DJ then announced that the bar was open, and that food would be served shortly.

I excused myself from the table.

With my small purse on my wrist, I held the bottom of the fitted ivory dress in my right hand as I headed to the ladies' room. I didn't have to use it, I just wanted to be alone, if only for a moment.

Once inside of the restroom, I glanced at myself in the mirror. Tatiana had done an amazing job on my makeup. I looked so pretty.

I opened my purse and pulled out my cell phone.

My feelings were all over the place. Maybe it was the occasion. Or perhaps it was because I was there alone.

I tapped on Nathaniel's number.

Since he was on my mind, I figured that it was time to return his phone call. I would rather hear whatever it was that he had to say from him, versus seeing something about it all over social media. I inadvertently stalked his social media pages, every other day. It used to be every day, a few times a day, but I was working on that though.

My nerves were all over the place as I listened to the ringing in my ear.

Voicemail.

He hadn't answered my call.

I didn't say anything, I just hung up. I knew that Nathaniel was going to call me back, but I held down the power button to turn off my phone anyway. I placed my cell phone back inside my small purse, and after fondling my curls for a while, I made my way back to the party.

"I guess this is one way to "bump" into each other again, huh? Although I was kind of hoping that you would call."

At the sound of his voice, I turned around to face him.

Sheriff Kori.

My brother.

Probably.

"It's not that. It's just…"

Should I tell him that I might be his sister?

I wasn't sure if it was my place. And most importantly, I guess I wasn't sure if it was true.

There were only two people that could say for sure, and one of them was dead; and as for the other, I couldn't be sure if he knew about me or what his version of the truth was since I'd been too afraid to ask.

"I just got out of a marriage. My divorce was finalized not too long ago and---I'm just not ready," I said, deciding that it was *his* father's job to break the possible news to him and not mine.

"Understood."

I watched Kori walk away.

He headed towards Marlo's husband, Luis, who was now up mingling with all of his friends. I assumed that he and Kori were probably pretty close buddies or something. I could tell by the look on Marlo's face when she saw them talking that she'd told her husband what grandma revealed to me that day, in front of all of them. She looked worried. As though she was hoping that her husband didn't let the truth slip out.

Marlo knew that she would have to deal with the *Wrath of Whinny* if he did.

Grandma was just like any other older person raised in the South during her time. She was old school, and their motto was simple: What happens in her house…what's said in her house…what's done in her house…stays in her house!

That's just the way she was.

The way that she'd always been.

And we'd been raised around so many others that felt the same way. Personally, though I'd followed the requirements growing up, now, and after a few years of therapy, I realized how damaging it was to your mental health not speak about situations that needed to be spoken of. Everything done behind closed doors doesn't have to *stay* behind closed doors. Sometimes it needs to be told. Sometimes it needs to be said. No matter how painful it may be.

Still, Marlo would get the cursing out of her life, at her own event, if grandma found out that she ran her mouth.

After my second drink, I finally started to relax, and I allowed myself to let my hair down. I danced a little, which I hadn't done in over a year; since the last time Nathaniel and I had gone out. And the drunker I became, the more fun I seemed to have. The only downside to the night was how hard I had to work to keep Kori from grinding on my booty; just in case he was my brother. Other than that, it was a fantastic night and a beautiful, drama-free event.

"You had yourself a good ole' time tonight," Roxanne laughed as she pulled up in front of the plantation house.

I'd been too drunk to drive me and grandma home.

Roxanne was the more religious of the group since her husband was a deacon at the church. They both refused to drink the *devil's nectar*, so she volunteered to take us home. Her husband trailed behind us. He was driving my car.

"I did. It was fun."

"Good."

"Grandma, I'm soooo drunk," I whined.

Roxanne chuckled loudly.

Grandma cursed me out the entire time as Roxanne's husband helped me up the front porch steps.

He gave grandma my car keys and then once he was in the car with Roxanne, she blew the horn as she started to reverse out of the driveway.

"Byyyeee Roxanne!" I yelled.

"Girl, shut the hell up 'fore you wake up the whole damn house!"

I burped. "Sorry, grandma."

"Come on," she helped me inside. She flipped on the light switch and as we moved slowly, my head boggled back and forth. I closed my eyes, but suddenly grandma stopped walking.

The house was so quiet.

"Grandma? I think I have to throw up," I called out to her with my eyes still closed.

She didn't respond.

She didn't move.

Struggling to lift my head, finally, I opened my eyes to look at her. I followed her eyes to the couch where she was staring at Gamma.

Gamma's eyes were wide open, and so was her mouth but even from a distance, you could tell that her body was stiff.

You could tell that Gamma...was dead.

~***~

I haven't been to a funeral in over fifteen years.

Mama's was my last one.

In New York, I hadn't dealt with much death. Nathaniel had a few distant relatives to pass away, but we hadn't gone to any of their funerals.

The coroner's said that Gamma's heart just stopped beating. They suggested that she'd probably been experiencing some tightness or that something wasn't feeling quite right for a few days. She just never said anything.

Now, it had been days since Gamma's death, and Grandma still wasn't saying much. I couldn't really tell if she was okay.

"Are you ready for the funeral tomorrow?" I asked grandma.

"If I can get this pot roast prepared and out of the way, I will be."

Grandma Whinny had been cooking nonstop all day.

Anything that you could think of, she'd cooked it. I saw ham, collard greens, and cornbread. Fish, turtle stew, and pinto beans. I even saw chitterlings, smoked chicken's feet, and a baked hen. And there was so much more.

And Grandma had cooked it all by herself.

I figured that cooking was her way of coping.

"Do you need any help?"

"No. I got it. Thank you."

She turned to face the kitchen sink, and after standing there for a few minutes with her completely ignoring me, finally, I turned to walk away. I glanced at the life insurance policy that she had sitting on the stand right next to the kitchen entrance.

She was Gamma's beneficiary.

The entire policy was going to her. I wondered how Aunt Pauline and Aunt Bertha Mae would feel about that. Even though grandma had been the one taking care of Gamma all of these years, they were still her kids too.

Grandma Whinny told me that she'd received a good bit of money from grandpa Bobby's insurance policy. I'd asked her that question when discussing Livy again. I'd wanted to know how she was able to afford to pay Livy's bills and she merely said that she had plenty of money that she didn't need. More than she would ever spend. She'd said that even before grandpa died they'd had plenty of savings. And Uncle Willie got a check too. And with Gamma's policy, she was about to come into a lump sum of cash again.

I decided to mind my business, and I exited the kitchen and made my way through the house. It was getting late and those who weren't staying the night were already gone.

I found Marlo on the front porch.

She and her husband decided to reschedule their ten-year anniversary trip because of Gamma's death.

"Some trip home, huh?"

I shrugged. "I guess." I sat down beside her.

"I'm thrilled that you're here. I missed you."

I smiled at her.

Marlo had changed drastically. She'd turned out completely different than I expected.

When we were younger, she was constantly handing out 'pussy passes' and screwing anything walking from here to Mississippi. Okay, so maybe I was exaggerating, a little, but let's just say she started early and she was what they called 'easy' back in the day.

She lost her virginity at only thirteen.

I know this because I was the first person she told. And every time after that, she told me too. It was like once she *popped*; she just couldn't stop. And she only got worse with age. She loved sex, with different people and she wasn't ashamed of it.

I remember around the age of seventeen when those little chat lines, the ones over the phone, had just started to pop up.

She would call them and pretend to be someone else. She would pretend to be older. She would even use a fake name. Most of the time she used the name: Charlene.

Anyway, she would find men, women, whoever---and she would talk to them. And after a few days of talking, she would sneak out and go meet them.

Nine times out of ten, she would have sex with them and then come home and tell me all about it.

She liked it.

She got a thrill out of it.

Thank God nothing ever happened to her.

I just knew that she was going to end up dead or locked up in a basement in the middle of nowhere, but she always came back home.

Marlo used to say that she thought she had a problem. She felt as though she liked sex too much.

I didn't see a problem with liking sex.

It was the 'random people sex' that was the problem.

Now, today, as I stared at her, she seemed so wholesome and sweet. It was as though that wild side of her never existed.

"A penny for your thoughts, shug?" Marlo asked.

"Nothing. I'm not thinking about anything," I lied.

I followed her gaze towards the men, and I took a second to examine Cassy's husband.

Cassy's husband, Corbin, was so damn sexy!

He was definitely that finest of the husbands; at least from the ones that I'd seen so far. From what they'd told me, he was born and raised in Alaska, but he was still African American. His parents were scientists and once they retired they moved to North Carolina. Corbin and Cassy met while he was in town visiting them and while she was out shopping with friends in Charlotte. They exchanged numbers and once he went back to Alaska, somehow, miles apart, and over the phone, they fell in love. Corbin is an engineer, and since his parents were already here, he took a job close by and moved here to be with Cassie. He married her shortly after that and not too long ago they'd had their first child.

Corbin had lighter skin, with short curly hair, but the best thing about him was his body. It had 'I'll fuck the shit out of you' written all over it, and it was something about the way that he smiled. That smile of his was dangerous. You couldn't stare at him for too long; unless you wanted to end up with a wet pair of panties. And not to mention that he was always in a suit. *Good Lord!* That made him all the more attractive to me.

I forced myself to stop looking at him, and I turned to see Marlo looking at me. She grinned.

"What?"

"He's *fine* as hell, ain't he?"

I shrugged.

How in the world did he fall in love with someone like Cassy?

Cassy was that cousin that was always mean for no reason. She always had something to stay. She always got spanked when we were growing up because she was always so nasty to people. I couldn't count the number of times I'd seen her slapped in the mouth as a result of back-talking. She was the very definition of *Negative Nancy*. She'd always been that way. And from what I could see, not much about her has changed.

I guess it's true when they say that there's somebody out there for everyone. Even for somebody like her.

"Do you ever wish that you would've stayed here?"

"Girl, hell no."

"Why did you go? Was it because of…"

I shook my head.

I knew what she was going to say, and I didn't want to talk about that. I didn't want to think about it either.

Marlo was the only one who knew one of my deepest, darkest secrets. I'd never told another soul. I hadn't told Nathaniel, and even though I've been going to my therapist for years, and even she didn't know the whole story. She just assumed.

"Marlo…"

"Okay," was all she said.

She changed the subject, and we spent the next hour or so, talking about random things. And then a few hours later, the house settled down, and people scurried around the house to claim where they were going to sleep.

I found grandma in Gamma's old room sitting on the edge of her bed.

"It's goin' be different 'round here without her. Always fussin'. Always cussin'."

I smiled at her as I sat next to her.

"Yeah. It'll be peaceful now."

Grandma Whinny chuckled. "Yeah." She looked towards the top of the bed. "She was as wicked as a person could be. Far from the perfect ma," she said.

"Is there even such a thing?"

Grandma shook her head.

"No, baby. I guess there isn't. Ahh, but growin' up with a ma like her took a lot of backbone. A lot of strength. Gamma was an evil woman. Just like her daddy. And I was her least favorite. Out of thirteen, she chose me to hate when I was just a youngin'."

"Why?"

"I don't know. I reckon it was 'cause I was different. I was very coy back then. I was nothin' like I am now. Nothin' like the way life made me. I wanted to learn. I wanted to know everything. I was rarely interested in anything that didn't teach me somethin'. I reckon she just didn't understand me. And people reject what they don't understand. She was raised to be mean and hateful. That's all she knew. Her daddy, my grandpa Ernest; that man was the devil himself. She hated him. But she turned out just like him. He ruined her. And in return, she almost ruined all thirteen of us too."

We'd heard many stories about our family history coming up. We'd heard some terrible things. Stories of disowning, beatings and even incest. Gamma always told us stories about everyone and everything; except for her daddy. I'd always known there was a reason why.

"I married yo' grandpa Bobby at a young age, just to get the hell away from her. Back then, we married young anyway, but I wasn't ready. I was just ready to get out of this house. And then, after I'd been married for a couple of years, she started to get sick. Daddy had been long *gone* by then, and it wasn't anybody here to take care of her. Yo' grandpa had just lost his job down at the old mill. So, with two small children and nowhere else to go, we came back home. My, my, my, I hated having to come back here. At first. When I left this house, I swore that I neva' would. I said that I would neva' come back. I didn't care if I ever spoke to her again. But here I was. Right back at home and we neva' left. Years past and wit' her health always up and down, she needed me. So, even after yo' grandpa went back to work, we decided to stay. Ha. The one she mistreated so much, ended up being all she had. Isn't that somethin'?" Grandma Whinny stood up. "Well, I'll see you in the *mawnin'*," she said incorrectly. Then she walked out of the room.

I exhaled loudly.

Looking around the room, there was so much white. The furniture, the curtains, and even the comforter on the bed was as white as picked cotton. She even had a dusty white bible next to the bed on her nightstand. You could tell that it hadn't been opened in years.

Gamma never allowed anyone to come into her bedroom. As a child, she would threaten to beat us if we so much as opened her bedroom door.

The room reeked of her scent.

I stood up and headed towards her white dresser.

I touched the photos in the frames. There were ten of them. One for each of her children that had passed away.

I had memories of some of them. Some I didn't remember at all. Some I'd never gotten to meet; like the two uncles that had died in wars.

Curiously, I tugged on the handle of her top drawer. I picked up one of her nightgowns just to take a whiff of it.

Death was hard for me.

Death reminded me of Mama.

Mama was....

She was a lot of things.

I couldn't say that she was a good mother, but she wasn't exactly a bad one either. She wasn't mean or hateful to me, but it was as though she didn't have much to give me. And I wasn't talking about material things. Time. Attention. Affection. Those little things from her were at a minimum. Rare. It was as though sometimes she forgot that I was there. Especially once I was old enough to fend for myself. Some days, she wouldn't come home, and I wouldn't see her for days at a time. We always lived here, in the house, so I guess she figured that I was okay. I wasn't. Some days, I just wanted her. She worked, but we never struggled or lived check to check. Grandma never required her to pay anything. Still, she didn't try to make her life better or travel the world. I hated how Mama acted as though *this* was enough. She never seemed to want anything more.

Mama was often criticized because she'd had a child without being married. At church, she couldn't hold a position. No one could if they had a child out of wedlock or was caught in any other kind of sin. They couldn't usher or sing in the choir if they had any 'open' sins, as they called them. They had to be redeemed first; which for Mama would've been for her to get married, but she never did.

I can remember her being ridiculed by her elders for not settling down and giving her child, me, a father. Strangely, mama never really seemed to care what they said about her and if she did care she never showed it.

Instead, she always told me that marriage wasn't something that you just do. It was something that you did on purpose. Something that you desired from the soul. And if it wasn't what I truly wanted then to hell with what anyone else had to say.

Maybe she'd meant it.

Or maybe she'd just been in love with a married man that she couldn't have. Maybe that's why she never married anyone else.

If Mama wasn't at work, then she was at the bar.

She had a drinking problem.

And what a nasty problem it was.

I'd seen her drunk just as many times as I'd seen her sober. As early as the age of ten I could remember rubbing her back as she leaned over the toilet to vomit. She always promised that she was going to stop, but of course, she never kept her word. No matter how many times she had to see the disappointed look on my face. No matter how many times she had to hear grandma's mouth about coming into the house drunk. She just couldn't seem to push the bottle away.

I didn't have a ton of bonding memories with her, but I did have a few. I had enough. Some of my favorite memories were of her singing to me. She could've been the next *Anita Baker*---Monday through Friday. And then she was all Aretha and full of soul on the weekends.

My God, I loved her voice!

I'd seen old videos of her singing in the church choir, before getting kicked out of it because she was pregnant with me. The whole church would rise to their feet as soon as she opened her mouth.

She could've been a singer. She'd had the talent. She just never had the dream. She never tried to be anything more than who or what she was.

Nevertheless, with all of her flaws and all of my failed expectations of her...I loved her. I loved her so much. She was my mama. The only one I'd been given. And she was taken from me, way too soon and before I was ready.

The night that I'd won homecoming queen, I couldn't wait to get home to tell her. She had to work that night and couldn't be there, but she'd helped me pick out my dress, and she'd helped me decide on what to do with my hair. She promised me that after work, she would come straight home just to hear about my night, but when I got back, she wasn't there.

I figured she'd ended up at the bar like always. I'd waited up for her that night, for a while, but I ended up falling asleep. The next morning, I went into her bedroom to find that she still wasn't there.

I had to babysit that morning, so I'd hoped she would be home when I returned.

She wasn't.

I'd come home to the painful truth that she would never be coming home again.

I closed the drawer, and I spotted the photo beside the door on a small table. It was a younger picture of Gamma. The photo was old. She had to be in her early twenties.

For the first time, ever, I could call her beautiful.

This is how I wanted to remember her.

I picked up the picture and placed it underneath my arm. No one would miss it. I was going to take it back home with me.

Before closing the bedroom door, I looked behind me one last time with a smile. And then, I looked up towards the roof of the house, as though I could see through it, and out into the night sky.

Goodbye Gamma. Tell Mama I said Hi.

The church was crowded and shoulder to shoulder, we snuggled against each other on the wooden bench.

Family and friends made their way around the casket. I sat there, staring at all of them, trying to put faces to names and memories.

I'd grown up in this church.

I'd spent so much time here when I was younger, mostly against my will. To this very day, I was sure that was why I didn't go to church. I'd overdosed on it back when I was young.

Grandma would make the whole house go to church. Tuesday Prayer. Wednesday Night Bible Study. Thursday Choir Rehearsal. Friday Worship. And then all-day Sunday, for at least two services, that's where I was.

I hated it.

I hated not being able to choose.

I'd meant to ask her why she hadn't been to church, not even once, until now since I'd been back in town. Maybe she finally realized that you didn't have to be in church every day to have a relationship with the Man Above.

I wished she'd felt that way when I was growing up.

The entire church hummed in unison the hymn, *I'm Free*, and I felt guilty for feeling relieved that no one was crying. Literally, no one, in the whole church was shedding a single tear.

Either everyone was at peace with Gamma's death because of her old age or they were happy that she was gone.

It was hard to tell.

The vibration of my cell phone startled me as my entire purse wiggled in between my feet.

It was probably Nathaniel.

He had the worst timing. We've been playing phone tag for the past few days, and still, I had no idea what he wanted to tell me; especially since he wouldn't do it over text message. I'd texted him and revealed to him that I was home in South Carolina. Instead of telling me what he had to say, he wanted to know why I was in the one place that I'd told him I hated.

I told him to mind his business.

Marlo elbowed me, and I turned my gaze towards her. She nodded her head towards Gamma's casket.

I followed her gawk, and she giggled softly, knowing that I'd seen what she wanted me to see.

Oh, Sweet Baby Jesus!

Is that him?

Yeah. That's him.

Damn, how tall is he?

Six-four? Maybe Six-five?

He had to weigh at least three hundred pounds, maybe more, but his height balanced it all out. His back was broad, and his arms were big, but he was in shape. And he didn't have the slightest belly. He probably had abs underneath his shirt.

Umm...

His skin had been kissed by the sun, and it reminded me of lightly burnt *Jiffy* cornbread. He had a nice, thick beard. He hadn't had one before, but of course, he was just a boy back then. Oh, but now...now he was all grown up.

Now, he was a grown ass man!

He turned from the casket searching for grandma to give her his condolences. And that's when he saw me.

Our eyes locked and time stood still. The look on his face was somewhere in between surprised and perplexed. Nervousness attacked me and not knowing what else to do, I lowered my head as he spoke to grandma.

Marlo elbowed me continuously, as his shadow past by me. I forced myself to wait a few seconds before looking up. Finally, I glanced behind me.

Instead of taking a seat, he strolled out the church, and it wasn't until the doors closed behind him that finally, I was able to breathe.

For the first time in fifteen years, finally, I'd seen his face.

My first kiss. My first love. My first everything…

Jace.

****

CHAPTER THREE

My first love.

That's what you are. That's what you will always be.

Seeing Jace had stirred up feelings inside of me that I hadn't realized were still there.

Maybe it was because we never got closure.

Maybe it was because I'd left without telling him goodbye.

I'll admit, I tried to forget him. And over the years, I somewhat had. But now, after seeing him, he seemed to be the only thing on my mind.

I had memories as far back as the age of seven with Jace in them. He was the Pastor's son, so we grew up in church together.

I was always there, and so was he.

For years he was a pest; like a little puppy chasing after a bone. He was always following me around. He was like a friend that I didn't have a choice but to have, and for a long time, I saw him as nothing more.

And then I grew up.

On my sixteenth birthday, I realized that I loved him.

He was standing there, talking to one of my cousins, but his eyes were on me. And I knew from the way that he looked at me that he loved me too.

He brought me a necklace for my birthday that year, and as he placed it around my neck, I decided right then and there that I didn't want to be his friend anymore. I wanted to be something more.

Later that night, as my birthday party came to an end, Jace found me outside on the tire swing. He brought me a piece of my birthday cake, and he asked me about my birthday wish.

I told him I wished for my first kiss.

I lied.

That hadn't been my wish, but with him standing right there in front of me, for some reason that's all I wanted to do. And I wanted to do it with him.

And I did.

That night, Jace towered over me with a smile, and then he lowered his head. He placed his right hand underneath my chin and brought my face closer to his. And then he granted my wish.

He kissed me.

And it was everything that I ever imagined my first *real* kiss to be.

After that night, our conversation was no longer friendly. It became something else. We became closer over the next few months and spent the entire summer together. And as we walked through the doors on the first day of our 11th grade school year, Jace grabbed me by the hand, and told everyone that I was his girlfriend.

And so, I was.

Jace became the star wide receiver on the football team, and I became the head of more clubs than I could keep up with. We quickly became Clover C. High School's favorite couple.

And he quickly became my favorite person.

Jace had always been the husky type.

By our senior year, he was at least six feet tall and well over two-hundred pounds. And he was very easy on the eyes. Attractive. Well-mannered and well-dressed. Most of the girls were jealous of me. And the few that weren't jealous of me wanted to be my friend.

For the most part, what Jace and I had was easy. We loved each other. We knew each other. We understood each other. And of course, our families approved of our relationship.

We thought that we would get married.

Everyone else thought the same.

Had it been up to Jace as soon as we'd turned eighteen we would've tied the knot. If we had, maybe I wouldn't have left.

We were both considered to be born late. Both of our birthdays were in November, so we'd started school a year after most, and we were always a little older than everyone else in our class.

We both turned eighteen, a week before the homecoming football game. On that birthday, Jace gave me a promise ring, but he made it clear that it could be more than just a promise. He'd said that it could be a reality. All I had to do was say yes.

Jace had scholarships all over the place for football, but he was refusing to accept any of them until I decided on a college. He'd wanted to see where I would get accepted. I had the grades. I was active in school. The teachers loved me. All I had to do was figure out where I wanted to go and start applying.

I never made it to that point. I didn't know that a week later my whole life would change.

After he gave me the promise ring, I finally decided to take our love to the next level.

I wanted to make love.

I'd forced Jace to wait, though he hadn't had a problem with it. For me, I hadn't known what would become of our relationship, at first, and I figured that if we didn't have sex, then it would be easier for us to go back to being just friends.

But I was done waiting. I just wanted him.

We were in his bedroom.

His parents were visiting another church, and they thought that he would be over at my house, but I'd talked him into letting me come to his.

Jace came over to my house often, but Grandma was old school. We couldn't shut my bedroom door, and she walked down the hall to look in on us what seemed like every five minutes. And she did it boldly, never tried to hide what she was doing. With his folks gone, we were all alone, and I made the first move.

Jace wasn't a virgin.

He'd had a girlfriend before me. Jace told me that they'd had sex a few times and that she was a lot more experienced than he was at the time.

So, I was nervous.

Nervous that I wouldn't do it right.

Nervous that he wouldn't enjoy it.

Luckily, it didn't take him long to take the lead.

He started to rub on me, kiss on me, and then...

"Vana?" Grandma Whinny snapped her fingers in my face. "Chile, what da' hell you thinkin' 'bout? I've been callin' yo' name for five minutes," she complained as I tugged on the top of my shirt. I fanned myself.

"Yeah, that's that 'I was thinkin' about dick' face," she chuckled. "I know that face," she mumbled as she made her way over to the kitchen sink.

The funeral had been a few days ago, and the family that had come into town was long gone.

Grandma was back to acting normal.

"How is yo' book coming along?"

"I haven't written in a few days. But coming back here has helped. Being here has brought back so many memories. Good and bad. Perfect for writing material," I huffed.

"Girl, you betta' not let me pick up that book and find it full of family business! No matter how old you are, I'll still *whip* yo' ass!"

And I was sure that she meant just what she said.

"I see you're still hangin' around here. I'm not complaining. I just thought you would've left the day after the funeral."

"That was the plan. I just wanted to make sure that you were okay."

"I'm gonna' be just fine. We live. We die. We just gotta' be ready. She was ready. I believe that. And her soul is where it's supposed to be. But anyway, since you're still here, do you mind runnin' by Livy's for me? I haven't been to check on her in a few days, with everything goin' on, and I like to make sure that she's holdin' up okay. You don't mind doin' that for yo' grandma, do you?" She batted her eyes.

I shook my head. "No. I don't mind."

Grandma gave me Livy's address and sent me on my way.

When thinking about Livy, I couldn't help but think about her stepdad, Harvey.

He was another reason why I'd left.

The biggest reason of all.

For years, I hadn't been able to say it aloud or accept it, but the truth is the truth; even when it's hard for you to face it.

Harvey raped me.

After mama died, Lord knows I was having a hard time.

Days were long. Nights were even longer.

Most days I just felt empty. I was always sad. I had family and friends trying to help me heal, but I just wasn't the same. I wasn't as focused in school as I had been before. I stepped down from my club positions. I did the bare minimum, and only what was required of me to maintain. College was no longer the main thing on my mind.

It was a tough time.

Jace had been right there. And when he couldn't be, there was Livy.

Livy was quiet and somewhat shy, except when she was around me. I guess since we'd been friends for so long. After losing mama, I'd needed her friendship more than ever before. And then there came a time when she needed me.

She wanted to go to the prom, but only if I went too.

She didn't mind being the third wheel with Jace and me. She said that she wanted the experience.

I was surprised that she wanted to go, but she said that she wanted the prom to be her best high school memory.

I didn't want to go. I mean, I really didn't want to go. I wasn't feeling all that social. I wanted to say no. I wanted to stay home and cry about mama. She couldn't see me off to the prom, so what was the point in going?

That's how I felt about it, but I put my feelings aside, and I decided to go for Livy. I got Jace onboard, though he'd said that it was okay with him if I hadn't wanted to go. I forced myself to get into the mood. I found a dress and together, the three of us went to the prom.

Livy was so beautiful that night.

Seeing her all dolled up was a sight to see. I'd never seen her show so much skin or have that much fun. She was so conservative. I was happy to see her come out of her shell, if only for one night.

Once the night came to an end, Jace drove us to Livy's house. She asked me to stay over. I wasn't really in the mood for prom night sex with Jace, so I agreed.

After Jace told me how beautiful I was, and that he was proud of me for getting out of the house and having a good time, he left me there.

He left me in *hell*.

Harvey was at home that night.

Livy's mama, Francesca, worked third shift at the time. Harvey was a barber. He owned the most popular barbershop in town, and everyone loved him. He was always doing something for the community and giving back. He was known for having a positive space where black men and young boys could go to relax, find help, or just to feel safe. He always gave high school students small jobs, and he had food at the barbershop, three times a week, to feed his customers or anyone else who may be hungry and looking for a hot meal.

He was respected.

He was one of our small-town heroes.

And he was a rapist.

I'd been around him for years, and nothing ever seemed off about him. He was funny and always cracking jokes. Always loving on Livy's mama, and Livy had never said anything bad about him. She always talked about her mom and how she was always trying to be the perfect wife, but she never had much to say about Harvey.

I remember the talk that Livy and I had that night. We'd talked about everything. We'd talked about the prom, and about how scary it was that high school was coming to an end. We'd talked about the future. Neither of us was sure about it, but both of us were afraid of it. We were afraid of what it might hold; we just assumed that we would be walking into it together.

Livy had applied to three colleges, but none were more than a few hours away from home. She said that even if I wasn't ready to go, she didn't want to be too far from me.

It wasn't that I wasn't ready.

I'd just lost focus at the time.

Livy fell asleep on me that night, and instead of sleeping in the bed with her, I went to sleep in the guest bedroom like I'd done so many times before.

I hated snoring, and Livy was the worst!

She snored so bad that if I didn't fall asleep before she did, I would be up the whole night nudging her to make her change positions.

After complaining one time in front of Mama Francesca, she told me that I could always sleep in the guestroom. And ever since she gave me the okay, when sleeping over most of the time that's where I would end up.

The hallway was dark that night, and Livy's parents' room door was closed. I'd tiptoed by it, and into the guest bedroom. I remember shutting the door behind me. I remember climbing into bed after taking off everything, except for my panties.

I was so tired.

Physically. Emotionally. Mentally.

I was drained, but at that moment, I remember feeling okay. I'd had a good night, and for the first time in a while, I just felt okay.

That didn't last long.

I can't remember when I dozed off, but I remembered getting a chill. With my eyes still closed, I searched for the covers that were somehow off of me, but I couldn't find them.

So, I opened my eyes.

And there he was.

Harvey.

He was standing over me.

It was dark; except for the glow of the moon seeping in through the spaces of the blinds. I couldn't see the expression on his face. However, I could tell that it was him.

And then I saw the whiteness of his teeth.

He smiled.

Knowing what he was about to do to me, that psychopath smiled.

I remember sitting up, hastily, still searching for the covers. I spotted them at the bottom of the bed, but when I pulled at them, Harvey snatched them from my hands.

"Harvey, what are you doing?" I'd asked him.

He didn't respond.

Immediately, I could feel that something was wrong.

I remember easing towards the edge of the bed, away from him. I glanced toward the bedroom door. It was wide open, even though I knew that I'd closed it. I was mostly naked. I wanted to cover my breasts, but I felt as though I would need my hands, so I didn't. Once the bottom of my feet touched the cold hardwood floors, my instincts told me to make a run for it.

I did.

I didn't get very far though.

I remember Harvey grabbing me by my hair and slamming me to the floor.

"Livy! Livy!"

I screamed so loud that my throat burned. It felt as though it was being torn into little pieces or as if it was being sliced with a knife. I started to kick my feet as Harvey made his way down to the floor next to me.

I tried to crawl away from him, but he grabbed my leg and pulled me back towards him.

"Livy!"

"Shut up!" Harvey threw a punch that even in the darkness, collided with my mouth.

The impact of the blow sent me into a state of shock, and just for a moment, I was stuck. The room started to spin, and the salty, distinct taste of blood in my mouth sent me into a state of panic. I screamed, swarmed, and tried my best to get out of Harvey's grasp.

"Livy!"

That night, Harvey placed his right hand around my throat and squeezed. I could barely breathe, but still, I scratched at his hand and peeled at his fingers as his left hand started to tug at my panties.

"No," I gasped as loud as I could. "No."

Harvey breathed heavily.

I prayed that Livy had heard me and that she would come in to help me. I prayed that the constant clawing would cause him to loosen his grip and that I would get another opportunity to try and get away from him.

But that never happened.

I never got away.

And help never came.

I remember the exact moment that I truly started to comprehend what was about to happen to me. I knew what Harvey was about to take from me. And then that sickening moment came. The moment where I felt him shove himself inside me. And it was at that moment that I stopped trying to catch my next breath. Breathing no longer mattered. Life no longer mattered. All I wanted to do was die.

I remember it all.

I remember how he slightly loosened his grip as he violated me, and that no matter how bad I wanted to cry I couldn't.

I couldn't do anything.

I couldn't feel anything.

I couldn't save myself from him. I couldn't stop what was happening to me. I've never felt so helpless. I've never felt so dirty and misused.

And the sounds.

The sounds from that night have haunted me for years. The way that Harvey breathed. The grunting noise that he made over and over again. The sound that his body made as he threw himself up against me. The sound of the old wooden floor as it creaked underneath me. It was as though the planks of the floor were weeping for me. I remember the sound of the train in the distance, as it whistled towards heaven on my behalf. And last but certainly not the least, I remember the sound of my breaking heart as it ripped into two. I remember thinking of how much I was already going through, and how heartbroken I was to have to add rape to the list.

I can't really say how long it lasted.

I just remember how I felt when it was over.

I remember feeling like my body wasn't my own.

And I remember his words.

"Thank you."

Thank me?

That's how I knew that he wasn't sorry for what he'd done to me.

It was as though he knew that there wouldn't be a consequence. And then he said:

"Unless you want to end up dead, just like your mama, I suggest you keep your mouth closed."

Dead like Mama?

I remember wondering if that meant he'd killed her and if he would really try to kill me too.

If I told.

Now, that I'm older, I realize that it was probably just a threat to buy my silence.

Or was it?

I couldn't be 100% sure.

Harvey left me, damaged and distraught on the bedroom floor. Once I was able to pull myself off of it, still unable to cry, I put on my dress, and slowly I made my way out of the room. Back in the hallway, I walked past the room that was occupied by the *devil*. I walked past the room where my best friend slept. I walked right out of the house, and out of her life.

Forever.

Ugh!

I started to breathe slowly, as I shook my head, wishing that I could shake my memories away. I hated to think about what happened to me. I hated to have to face my truth. And most of all, I hated Harvey.

On the other side of town, I couldn't quite remember all of the roads, so I followed the GPS towards the address that grandma had given me. I headed towards Livy's house.

As I drove, I took in my surroundings. I hadn't been on this side of town since I'd been back, and there were a lot of things and businesses that I didn't recognize.

A lot of buildings from my childhood were missing, but I saw that one building was still standing and business was still booming as I drove by it.

Harvey's Barbershop.

It was still there.

Just for a few seconds, fear entered my body and filled the empty spaces of my heart.

I've only told one person the truth about Harvey, and what he did to me that night. I told Marlo.

After the violation, I left Livy's house and walked all the way home. It was only about a ten-minute drive but walking, it'd taken me about forty-five minutes. The house was dark when I got home, and I thought that everyone was asleep. It wasn't until I made it to my bedroom that the pain of my reality sunk in, and I wept from the deepest part of my soul.

I remember holding my mouth and biting down on my pillow to silence my cries. I didn't want anyone to hear me. I didn't want to make too much noise, and I didn't want anyone to know that I was hurting.

I was ashamed and embarrassed, and though I knew that I hadn't done anything wrong, I couldn't shake off the feeling that maybe it had happened because of me.

And then my bedroom door opened.

My heart dropped, thinking it was grandma. I was scared because I didn't know what I was going to say, but it had been Marlo.

"So, how was the prom?"

Her smile instantly disappeared from her face once she noticed the tears.

"What is it? What the fuck did Jace do?" She'd asked.

She held me and let me cry on her shoulder for a long while, and then she asked me again what was wrong.

And...and...I told her.

Marlo was furious and demanded that I tell someone, and she tried to make me call the police, but I told her that I couldn't. I didn't tell her about the threat that Harvey had made. I just told her that I didn't want anyone to know. I told her that I was ashamed.

Marlo didn't understand.

She wanted justice. She wanted Harvey to pay for what he'd done to me, but I was afraid.

What if he made good on his word?

Or worse...what if no one believed me?

What if everyone took his side instead of mine?

What if he lied and told everyone that I wanted it?

My mother hadn't had a good reputation. She'd often been referred to as a Jezebel. A fornicator. A whore.

What if they called me the same?

I had to beg Marlo to stay quiet, reminding her that I was the vault that held all of her secrets and transgressions. I pleaded with her to let me get through the pain in my own way. I begged her to let me forget. And although I knew that I would never forget what happened to me, I just couldn't imagine how I would've felt if the whole town found out about it.

If Jace found out about it.

Marlo let it be known that she didn't like my decision, but she gave me her word that she would keep my secret. Then, in silence, she helped me tend to my swollen mouth, and then she followed me into the bathroom and put me in the bathtub.

Neither of us said another word.

All I could do was cry. Marlo cried too.

The barbershop disappeared from my rearview mirror, and I exhaled. One day he was going to pay for what he did to me.

Barely paying attention to the road from being lost in my thoughts, somehow, I still managed to make it to Livy's house.

It was a little house, tucked neatly at the end of a dirt road. Grandma had found the house for her and had been covering her rent. Rent in Clover, South Carolina was nothing like rent in New York. Grandma told me that the house that Livy lived in was only about $400 a month. Grandma could afford it, but I told her that I would write her a check for Livy's rent before I left. All she would have to do is cash it, and just pay Livy's rent with it each month.

I was going to try and convince Livy to go to rehab. Though she hadn't been able to save me that night from Harvey, maybe I could save her.

And though I'd completely cut her off, along with everyone else, I never actually blamed her for what happened to me.

Harvey was the only one to blame, but honestly, everyone else paid the price.

I barely spoke to anyone after that night. I was barely making it from day to day. Graduation day came that next weekend, and I remember barely wanting to go.

Grandma knew that something was wrong with me, and she had been nagging me so much that eventually, I snapped on her; which had unquestionably been the wrong move.

Grandma slapped the graduation cap off of my head and told me that she would kick my ass if I ever screamed at her again. And then she dragged me out of the house, literally, and pushed me into the car. She fussed the entire drive to the high school, and up until I got out of the car.

Jace and Livy had been waiting outside for me at the school, but I'd walked right past them, as though they weren't there.

Both of them chased behind me.

Jace had touched my arm, and I snatched it away from him. I remember the look on his face before I turned my back to him. He was confused. Sad. I knew that he didn't understand, but I couldn't tell him what was wrong with me.

As we waited for the ceremony to start, I didn't say anything to anyone. I cried the entire time that I stood in line, and as I walked across the stage to get my diploma. I didn't take my seat with the others or wait to toss my hat into the air. With my diploma in my hand, I just kept walking. I walked out of the building.

Jace came out behind me.

He begged me to talk to him. He wanted to know what was wrong, but I couldn't say anything. He kept trying to touch me and each time I flinched, he cursed at me. He thought that it was something that he'd done. He thought that he had done something wrong.

He hadn't.

And I couldn't open up my mouth to tell him that it wasn't him. I wanted to. I really did. I wanted to tell him that it wasn't his fault. And I wanted to tell him that I loved him, but I said nothing. Jace stormed off, and I didn't call out to him. I didn't do anything. That was the last time I saw him; until the other the day at the funeral.

Grandma called me everything but a child of God once she came outside. She told me that she was disappointed in me, and she said that the way I was acting was embarrassing and ridiculous. She thought that it had something to do with mama. At the core, maybe it somewhat did.

She was so upset that she called off my graduation party, but I didn't care. I just wanted to be left alone.

Once back home, I stayed in my room for the rest of that day. I didn't eat. I didn't talk to anyone.

Grandma kept coming into the room to nag and complain, but I never responded to her no matter what she said.

And then the next morning, I woke up, knowing that if I didn't go, that if I didn't leave, I was going to die.

Or much worse...I would've ended up just like Livy.

I had to get out of there. I just had to go.

And I'm so glad I did.

Once I reached Livy's front door, I knocked on it. I waited for a while, and once she didn't answer it, I turned the knob, knowing that it was probably unlocked.

It was.

"Livy?"

I walked inside.

Surprisingly, the house was clean.

Probably because of grandma.

She told me that every time she brought food over, she made sure to tidy up and wash Livy's clothes.

I'd asked her how bad off Livy was, and grandma said that things with Livy could be worse. She was on drugs, but grandma felt that her having food, and a place to come home to made things a lot better than they could be. She didn't have to sleep on the street or do things that she didn't want to do for her next meal. She just had to make it home.

"Livy?"

I found her on the couch, with the needle still in her hand. The sight of her caused me to put my hand over my heart as though touching my chest would stop it from aching.

"Livy?"

She was spaced out. Her eyes were bulging, as she stared off into the distance.

"Hey, I just came by to check on you."

She didn't say anything.

I'm not sure if she even knew I was there.

Plates with old food on them were all over the table, along with lots of photos. I picked up a few of them.

They were of her, her husband, and their daughter. Her daughter had looked just like her.

Livy was brown-skinned, with a rather unique look. She wasn't an ugly girl. Her look was just different. And before the drugs, her body had always been one to die for. Livy used to be stacked like pancakes. Her body had been proportioned just right. She used to have curves for days, even though she always tried to hide them.

"He took everything from me," she slurred.

"Who?"

She didn't look at me.

"I miss them."

"I know."

Finally, she looked at me.

"You look like a friend I used to have back in the day. Her name was Savannah."

What?

Livy gave me a small smile. She was as high as a kite.

"I am Savannah, Livy."

"No. Savannah left me. Savannah is gone. Just like everyone else."

"No. I'm right here Livy."

Livy started to sob.

"I just want my baby back. I want my husband back. I want my family. I just want my family!"

Livy attempted to do something with the needle, but I walked over to her, and I took it out of her hand. She tried to take it back from me, but I threw it across the room. And then I flopped down on the sofa beside of her and pulled her close to me.

"You're going to be okay, Livy."

I forced myself not to cry.

"Nothing is going to be okay. I don't have anyone."

"You have me."

She didn't respond.

I wasn't sure if I was making a promise that I couldn't keep.

"The only one that deserved to die is Harvey. Harvey should've died. Not mama. Not Sajohn. Not Leah. Just Harvey."

"Why Harvey?" I asked her.

"Why not? After everything he did to me. After all the nights that mama was at work, and he came into my room."

What? Wait a minute…did Harvey rape her too?

It had never crossed my mind before. Partly because Livy had never spoken badly about him while we were growing up. She always seemed to love him. Although she thought her mother loved him *too* much, if there is such a thing, she never seemed to have an issue with him.

"I didn't like it. I never liked it. But I didn't have a choice. The first time I was fifteen. He's the only father I've ever known. But *fathers* aren't supposed to want to have sex with their daughters."

Oh no!

Livy's real dad died a few months after Livy was born. A tragic work accident.

"I tried to tell mama. So many times. I just didn't know how. I didn't know what to say. She loved him so much. I knew that it would break her heart if she knew the truth about him. If she knew the truth about her precious husband. If she knew..."

I was anxious to hear what she was going to say next.

"He was so jealous. So jealous of me. He didn't want me to date. He didn't want me to show my body. He didn't want anyone else to want me. He wanted me all to himself."

The anger that I felt. The pain that I felt. I just couldn't describe it. It happened to her. The same thing that had happened to me...had happened to her.

And all the time.

She hadn't told me, just like I hadn't told her.

I wished that one of us had been brave enough to tell the someone that could help or the police, and I couldn't help but to think that if she'd said something then just maybe it would've never happened to me. Maybe Harvey would've never raped me.

"Even on my wedding day, Harvey saw me going into the bathroom and he followed me. I didn't know who had come in behind me until I came out of the stall. And there he was. Standing in front of the bathroom door with it locked behind him. He taunted me. He questioned me. He asked me if I liked my husband's dick better than his. I never liked his. I never wanted his. And I hated that he wanted me. And on the most important day of my life, he wanted me again. I tried to push past him, but he said that he wanted *it* just one more time. I begged him to leave me alone. To just let me enjoy my day. To just let me be."

Livy pulled away from me.

"He tried to rip my dress. Told me that either I was going to lift it up and give myself to him or he was going to rip it off of me and take it. He'd controlled my mind and my tongue for so long that the obvious things to do didn't appear to be options. But thankfully, I had a husband who had come looking for me. As Harvey stared at me, a knock came to the bathroom door. My new husband yelled out my name and knocked over and over again. I yelled back to him. The look on Harvey's face when I opened my mouth could've sliced me into a thousand pieces, but for the first time, I felt in control. With a smirk on my face, Harvey moved from in front of the door and hid in one of the stalls. After fixing my dress, I opened the door in a hurry and greeted my new husband with a forced smile. I lied to him. I told him that I'd had a slight wardrobe malfunction and had been trying to fix it. He didn't question me. He took my word, and then took me by the hand. And for the first time, I had someone to protect me. I knew right then that Harvey would never hurt me again."

Livy exhaled.

Open your mouth, Savannah.

Tell her that it happened to you too.

"After that day, I never went over to mama's house. I always made her come to mine. I never told Sajohn the truth about Harvey, but he could tell that it was something off about him. He'd said that he had everyone else fooled, but that he could see right through him. He was right. The beloved barber was…and probably still is…a rapist."

Livy started to look from side to side, as though she was looking for something. When she couldn't find it, she just sat there. I waited to see if she would say something else, but she didn't. She didn't say another word.

Silently, she sat and just stared.

And I sat beside her and did the same.

Poor Livy.

~***~

"Are you my father?"

I couldn't leave without knowing the truth.

After hearing Livy's confession, I'd had enough of the South. I'd gone back to the plantation house, and after getting my things together, I wrote until the sun came up. The pages that I'd written were full of regret and despair. And so was I. I had so many regrets. I had so many things that I wished that I could change. Unfortunately, I couldn't change the past, but I was in charge of my present. And it was time that I start acting like it.

"Excuse me, young lady?"

"My mother was Glorianne Lynch."

The expression on his face told me all that I needed to know. He looked at me. As though he was trying to see himself *in* me. He studied my face for a resemblance.

"I'm sorry....uh...you have the wrong man. Now, if you'll excuse me," he said as he brushed past me.

What?

"I know that you're my father. I just wanted to meet you. I've always just wanted to meet you."

The man didn't turn around to face me.

"You have a good day now, okay," he said over his shoulder.

I swallowed the lump in my throat. I stared at the back of him for a while, hoping that he would turn around.

He didn't.

I pushed my disobedient curls behind my ears, I tugged at the bottom of my jean jacket, and then I headed towards the door.

I tried.

"Savannah?"

It had been years since I'd heard his voice. And although his voice was deeper, it still had a familiar tone.

I exhaled softly, and then I turned around to face him.

Jace.

I was surprised that I hadn't spotted him in the store as soon as I'd come in. And then again, I hadn't been paying attention. My only focus had been on locating and approaching the owner.

Jace had a hand full of tools as he walked closer to me.

Timid, I examined him from top to bottom.

He was wearing a gray fitted cap and a plain white t-shirt. It was gray sweatpants season, so instinctively, my eyes made their way down towards the center of his pants. I cleared my throat as I pulled my eyes away from the print and back to his face.

Jace stared into my eyes as though he was trying to read my mind.

"I—uh—I wish I'd been able to hang around for the end of the funeral to catch up with you, but I had something that I had to do," he said.

He was massive. He was like one big, sexy ass giant.

And I couldn't stop looking at his tatted, oversized arms.

I'd thought of him a few times in the past. Quite a bit when I first left. I remember wondering why I'd never seen him on T.V. as a football player. I loved football. And I'd been sure that Jace was going to make it to the league. I was curious to know why he hadn't.

"I'll never forget that day."

"What day?" I managed to say.

I could see the man that was supposed to be my father continuously glancing at me in curiosity.

"The day I went by your grandma's house. The day that you disappeared. I waited there for you all day. You never came home. I called the next day, and your grandma told me that you weren't coming back. She told me that you called her and told her that you were never coming home. That whole summer, I stayed home. I waited by the phone. I just knew that you were going to call me. And say something. You know, say anything. But you never did. You never called."

"Jace---"

My mouth was dry.

Just then, Sheriff Kori walked into the store.

"Hi," he said to me immediately, as though he didn't see Jace standing there.

I looked past him at Jace, and he looked back at him.

"How are you doing man?" He said to Jace and Jace nodded his head.

"I see you're still around," Kori said.

"Not for long. I'm about to leave."

I noticed the look on Jace's face.

"Oh. Okay. Well, if you don't…the number on the card is still the same. If you want to have a drink or anything," he said. I could tell that he wasn't used to hearing no, but screw it, I was about to tell him why I couldn't go out on a date with him.

"Well…I may be using the number after all," I said to him.

Kori smiled, but I continued. "To call you and ask you about what *our father* said about me."

Hell, I may as well try to get the truth out of him. One way or another.

Kori looked confused.

"Apparently, your dad…is my dad too. So, I've heard."

I left Kori standing there, with a dumbfounded look on his face as I walked out of the hardware store.

Seconds later, now empty-handed, Jace came out the door behind me.

"Are you serious? Is he really your dad?" He asked me.

"Yeah. Really. At least that's what grandma said."

Jace knew, more than anyone, how much I'd wanted to meet my daddy. He knew how important it had been to me back then.

It was chilly, and I shivered as a cool breeze lingered in between us. It was early October, and I started to have slight memories of how the town looked during the holidays.

"Why did you leave me?"

Jace interrupted my thoughts.

I looked at him.

"What did I do? Why did you push me away?"

I guess I could somewhat explain. I owed him that much.

"I had to go Jace."

"Why?"

"I just had to."

He bit his bottom lip.

Oooh.

"Um, Jace...it wasn't you. It didn't have anything to do with you. It was just something that I'd had to do for me. You were perfect. I loved you and---"

"I love you."

"What?"

"I never stopped loving you, V."

He used to call me V as a pet name, for whatever reason. I guess since some called me Vana, he'd decided to call me V.

"I thought about you all the time. I always asked about you. I know you're married now and what not, but..."

"I'm divorced."

Jace chuckled. "Me too."

He'd gotten married?

To who?

Probably some church girl.

"So, you're leaving?"

"Uh, yeah. Maybe today."

Jace nodded his head and placed his hands in his pockets. He looked at me and bit his bottom lip again before he muttered his next words. "So…what can I do to make you stay? At least for another day? Come on V, stay. Just give me a day." His smile made my knees buckle.

I tried to collect my thoughts, and then I smiled at him flirtatiously. "Well…since it's you…I guess giving you a day is the least I can do."

Uh oh. Savannah…what are you getting yourself into?

****

CHAPTER FOUR

"You told me that you were thinkin' about leavin' three days ago," Grandma grinned at me slyly. "You stickin' 'round here wouldn't have anything to do with the Pastor's boy, now would it? I saw y'all outside the other day."

"No," I huffed. "I'm still leaving. I just…"

"Um huh," Grandma cut me off. I watched her as she rolled the dough over and over again.

"Couldn't get you to come back here for years. Now, fate can't get you to leave."

Fate?

Is that why I'm still here?

Being around Jace for the past three days had my feelings all out of whack. Whenever I was in his presence, part of the time I was filled with regret, and maybe even a little bit of worry. And then the other half of the time I was wrapped in comfort, relaxed, and consumed with laughter.

Jace was a lot funnier than I remember.

I was smiling with him more than I had in the past year. And honestly, it felt good.

Not to mention, that it was surprising.

Surprising that after all of these years, we still had some type of connection.

Jace and I had spent the entire first day reminiscing and talking about everything underneath the sun.

And I met his daughter. She was eight, and so pretty too.

Her name was Yasmine.

Jace explained that he had gone to college after I left. He'd attended Clemson State University, and in the last game of his freshman year, he injured his knee. Things weren't as advanced as they are these days, and with a shattered knee, Jace was forced to face a sad reality. His dreams of making it to the league were over. Devastated, Jace dropped out of school, came back home, and after feeling sorry for himself for a while, he pulled himself together and decided to go to barber school.

Jace was now a barber. And he worked for Harvey.

And the worst part of all was that Jace looked at Harvey through eyes of admiration, just like everyone else in this town. He had no idea the type of man that he'd been associated with all of these years, and every time that he said his name, I wanted to scream.

Jace told me that Harvey was about to retire and that he was days away from buying the barbershop. They were in the process of finishing up the paperwork.

Apparently, Jace was the go-to guy for haircuts these days. The other day, his phone rang at least ten to fifteen times with people trying to set up appointments to get a fresh cut. And he was charging $25 a head; so, the money could surely add up. And considering that he was driving a Mercedes G-Class SUV, I guess the money had been adding up for quite some time.

Owning a barbershop was definitely the right---best next move for him. Jace stated that he was leaning towards opening a barbershop in a bigger city, like Charlotte, but when Harvey told him that he was ready to retire and sell, he couldn't pass up his offer. So, he was buying the barbershop. And he had some pretty good ideas on how to bring in even more business, so I was happy for him.

I still wished that Harvey was dead.

Jace's parents still had the little white church on the corner, right in the center of what we called *the block*. It still had the small creek behind it and everything. I found it funny that they hadn't expanded or built on to the church. The church has had a "building fund" since I was five...but there damn sure hasn't been any building going on!

Jace told me that grandma stopped going to church years ago. He'd heard rumors about grandpa, and another woman at the church, but he wasn't sure if they were true.

Hmm.

Grandma told me about grandpa Bobby's affair, but she didn't tell me that the woman, whoever she was, had gone to the same church. Now I see why she doesn't go to the church anymore.

I was surprised to learn that Jace had moved out of Clover. He lived in another small town called Mount Holly; which was technically in North Carolina. Not too far from Charlotte. Still only about thirty-minutes from Clover, and the barbershop.

Mount Holly was where his ex-wife was from, and where she still lived. Her name was Reeva.

He said that they met one night at a gas station. He called her beautiful. Smart. Funny. And he said it didn't take him long to fall in love with her. They married two years after they started dating, and not long after that, they had their daughter. And then, they had a son. According to Jace, they had a good marriage, up until their son died.

He was four months old when he passed away from SIDS. Jace said that early one morning, she wondered why he hadn't woken them up to be fed, and when she went into the nursery to check on him---he was *gone*.

He'd passed away.

Jace said that he could still hear her painful shriek from that day, from time to time inside his head.

Losing their son was devastating.

It hurt them. It changed them.

And it tore them apart.

Jace said they tried to heal together, but every day they grew further and further apart until they agreed that a divorce was the best solution for both of them.

Jace stayed in Mount Holly to be close to their daughter, and to accommodate their co-parenting schedule.

I loved how he treated his daughter. He treated her like a princess. I could tell that there was nothing in the world that he wouldn't do for her. And it made me remember how he used to treat me.

Jace and I were young, but Jace had been raised by old, Christian folks. He was dominant, manly, but he believed that a woman was his *favor* from God. That a woman was one of the best things that could happen to a man.

And it showed.

He was a big country boy and had always treated me with the utmost respect. He opened doors and pulled out chairs. He didn't have a problem with communicating or expressing his feelings. He would shower me with compliments on a daily basis, and he wouldn't pass on an opportunity to show me that he loved me. He loved hard. He loved me so much. And he wasn't afraid to show it.

I thought that we were going to be together forever.

And then when Mama died, I changed.

He'd tried to love me, in spite of, but I was going through something. I was trying to sort through my feelings. And to do that, I'd had to shut him out. I thought that it would only be for a while, and then the rape happened. And nothing else really mattered to me after that.

Not even him.

On the day I ran away, Jace didn't even cross my mind. I didn't think about him until I was sitting in the pancake house, the next night, thinking about what I'd done. Still, I couldn't force myself to call him.

What was I supposed to say?

Goodbye?

I guess that would've been the right thing to do, but I just didn't want to hear his voice. I didn't want to break his heart. Well, I ended up doing that anyway.

"Hmmm, you're quiet. Must be thinkin' 'bout that boy," Grandma chuckled, reminding me that she was there.

"I was wondering why you didn't go to church every day like you used to. Jace told me that it was because of the rumors about grandpa and the affair."

"Jace talks too much," she mumbled. "And he's right. But it wasn't the woman that I told you about. It was another one."

"What? Really?"

"Yes. I'd seen them flirting a time or two, so I asked him, and he told me that they'd fooled around a few times."

"He told you?"

"He always told me. She'd been runnin' her mouth that's how it got around the church. Folks were always whisperin' when I came around. So, I just stopped comin' around. I stopped goin' to church."

"I'm so sorry grandma. I'm sorry that grandpa did those things to you."

"Oh chile, don't be sorry for me. Be sorry for them. And their souls."

I nodded. "Do you need some help?"

Grandma was cooking Sunday dinner.

She was making a ham, neck bones and rice, fried okra, sweet potatoes, and homemade biscuits.

"I can manage. Go on, invite Jayceon over for Sunday dinner."

I smiled at her and did as I was told.

An hour or two later, the house was filled with so much laughter and love. There were family members all over the place, and it was moments like these that I hadn't realized that I missed so much, until being back here.

I smiled from the window as I watched the children running around the backyard and then I turned my attention back to the card table.

They were playing spades. I hadn't played in years.

Grandma Whinny and my cousin Eve were playing against Marlo and Cassy. They were talking to each other as though they were strangers off the street. Taunting and nitpicking, and a curse word or two, here and there.

The men were piled in the living room, yelling at the T.V. Football was on, and Uncle Willie kept coming in and out of the kitchen to get beers. Grandma would fuss at him, whenever she noticed him, saying that he'd better not be drinking since he was on his medicine. I chuckled every time he walked down the hallway, before taking a sip.

This was life.

This was family.

I still had my bags packed in a corner, in the back bedroom, but every day, I was finding a reason to stay. And for right now, my reason was Jace.

"What's up, Jace!" I heard Marlo yell, and I looked behind me.

He smiled at me.

"Dammmmnnnn! He's so damn *fine*!" Cassy muttered.

"Corbin! You better come and get your wife!" My cousin Tatiana yelled with a smirk.

"What? Hell, y'all know he looks good. I ain't seen him in a while," Cassy shrugged.

"He was at the funeral Cass," Marlo said.

"Oh. I didn't see him."

Grandma laughed. "Hell, how could you miss him?" She winked at Jace. "Hello, Jayceon. I'm glad you could stop by."

Jace finally made his way over to me and held out his arms. I walked into them.

"Ooooh!"

The room filled with cheering, and chants as he embraced me.

I blushed.

"Do you want something to drink?"

"Nah. I'm alright."

"Wanna' go outside and chat for a second?"

Jace nodded.

I grabbed his hand, and lead him out of the kitchen, with all kinds of assumptions and sarcastic remarks being thrown at us from behind.

Once we were outside on the porch, I attempted to take a seat, but before I could, Jace pulled me closer to him again.

"Hey."

His big luscious pink lips curved up into a smile.

"Hey."

I was short, only about 5'4" so even with me standing on my tip-toes, it seemed to take him forever to come down to my level and rub his nose against mine. His beard tickled my face, causing me to giggle.

We didn't kiss, but I could tell that we both wanted to.

"I see you're still here."

"Yeah. I am."

"Why?"

"I don't know."

"I know."

"Oh yeah, so why? Why am I still here Jace?"

"Because I'm here. And you're feeling everything that I'm feeling. About us. I know you are."

"Cocky?"

"No. Hopeful."

"Hopeful about what?"

"About you. About you and me."

Jace had never been afraid to express how he felt. That was one of the things that I loved about him. After smiling and staring at each other for a few more seconds, finally, Jace released me and allowed me to sit in one of the rocking chairs. He sat in the one next to me.

"What's New York like, anyway?" He asked.

"Nothing like here," I chuckled. "Manhattan is busy. Crowded. Tight. And loud. Well, for the most part. I live in the suburbs, so when I go home at night, I have a little peace. Still, life is a lot slower here compared to there. There--- there never seems to be enough hours in a day. Here, the days take too long to end."

The orange and yellow leaves rustled, and a few of them gracefully fell to the ground.

"Maybe I'll have to come and visit you someday."

"Maybe."

Jace looked at me as though he wanted to lick my face.

"You're so beautiful."

"Jace, stop," I blushed.

"You are. Even with that big grandma-looking hat on," he chuckled.

"Uh, I like my hat! It's cute," I laughed.

"If you say so."

We shared another chuckle, and then we were quiet for a while. It was windy, and we both seemed to be admiring the swaying branches and falling leaves.

"I uh, we'll be finishing up the paperwork tomorrow. Tomorrow morning, the barbershop will be mine. I'll be the new owner."

"Good! I'm happy for you. And please tell me that you're changing the name," I rolled my eyes.

"I am. New name. New set-up. New services. Some new employees. All that."

"Uh oh, I'm scared of you," I teased. "Mr. Business Owner, and all."

Jace chuckled and then sat back in the chair. He separated his knees. I tried not to glance down, but I couldn't help it.

"Shit, go on and touch it then."

"What?" I looked at him embarrassed.

Jace just laughed and shook his head.

"So, when are you going to let me take you out on a real date?"

"I've been hanging out with you for the past few days."

"I know. But we haven't been on a date."

I shrugged.

"Our birthdays will be here soon."

"Oh no. I'll be gone way before then."

"Will you?"

"Yes."

"Okay then. Well, what about Friday night?"

I grinned at him. "You want me to stay here for almost another week?"

"Why not? I'll make sure it's worth it," Jace stared at me seductively.

For a while, I just looked at him, as he looked at me. Finally, I exhaled with a grin.

"I might stay until Friday."

"Oh, you might, huh?"

Jace stood up and walked over to me. He reached for my hands and started to pull me to my feet. Once I was standing in front of him, he lifted my hat and kissed my forehead. And then he hugged me.

Tightly.

"Fifteen years and I'm still crazy about you," Jace said.

That part was obvious.

"Why? After I left you. You should be angry with me."

"Nah. Sometimes you just have to let shit go."

I wish it were that simple for me.

Suddenly, Grandma Whinny yelled my name, and with Jace following behind me, we headed back inside.

"Yes?"

"Come and fix him a plate," she said, just as Uncle Willie walked into the kitchen.

"Some white man is at the door," he said to grandma.

She started to mumble and walked out of the kitchen just as I grabbed a plate.

Jace came as close as he could to me from behind, and then he started to tell me what he wanted me to put on his plate. I was finding it hard to focus with his *junk* on my *trunk* and I tried not to show that I was getting aroused. It had been a long time since I'd been touched---well since I'd been touched by someone else, and there wasn't a woman alive that wouldn't want to be touched by him. I tried to move away from his penis, but he kept coming closer.

The kitchen suddenly filled with chatter, and I turned around to see what all the fuss was about. My heart dropped once I noticed him standing next to grandma.

I opened my mouth, but nothing came out.

What in the hell is my ex-husband, Nathaniel, doing here?

~***~

"She died."

I stared at Nathaniel, unsure of what to say.

He showed up out of nowhere yesterday.

I didn't even know that he knew that much about me to know where to find me. Of course, I'd told him that I was from Clover, but that was pretty much it. Everything else, he'd found out all on his own.

Yesterday, Nathaniel introduced himself to everyone, and then he asked to speak to me outside. Slowly, I followed him out of the kitchen, with whispers behind me, and without looking back at Jace.

Once outside, Nathaniel stated that he'd come to talk to me, since I didn't appear to be coming home anytime soon. Nathaniel told me that he could see that I was busy and that he was staying in a hotel, not far from the house. He said that he didn't want to impose, but that the next day, we needed to talk.

So, here we were.

The next day.

Talking outside the hotel.

Nathaniel was so many things all rolled into one. Sometimes, he was one of those white boys who wore flip-flops and shorts in the wintertime and loved country music. And other times, he dressed down with jeans, a pair of Jordan's and he could recite the lyrics to any rap song, without missing a beat.

And he was so freakin' professional too.

He was tall, tanned, full of intellect and suave. He looked damn good in a suit, but even better in khakis, a collared shirt and Sperry's, and he was so attractive and charismatic that any woman, of any color, in any room, would hope and pray that he looked her way.

Standing in front of me he wore navy blue casual pants and a pale-yellow button up shirt. His head was shaved bald, and his beard had gotten huge. He wore the Rolex that I'd gotten him two Christmas's ago on his wrist.

"She died. And the baby died too."

"Nathaniel---I---"

"The doctors said that it was nothing that they could do. A pregnancy complication. She was only thirty weeks. She wasn't due, but she wasn't feeling well, so she went to the hospital. Her blood pressure was so high, and they found a blood clot. Everything that could've gone wrong did, and they wanted to do an emergency C-section. They weren't sure if they would be able to save them both, but she'd asked them to save the baby if they had to choose. She wouldn't listen to my opinions on the matter, and then they rolled her away. Sadly, they weren't able to save either of them. You know, standing there and hearing that both of them were gone, I was sad, devastated, but for some strange reason, I started to think about you. I couldn't help but think…what if that had been you? As much as I'd pressured you for a baby. I thought there was nothing more important than giving me what I wanted, not realizing that there were so many things that could've gone wrong. I would've never forgiven myself if something like that had happened to you. If that'd been you. If you had died because of me. Because I wanted a baby."

Wait a minute. What's that look?

Nathaniel looked at me with…

Love?

"I didn't love Nada. She was a fun night that happened to get pregnant. I cared for her, deeply, and appreciated her for the gift and child that she was going to give to me, but I didn't love her. I love you. Savannah, divorcing you, and leaving the way that I did was the biggest mistake that I've ever made."

What!

My stomach was in knots, and I had no idea what he was going to say next.

"And if it's not too late…" Nathaniel reached for my hand. "I just want you back. I want the love of my life back."

Oh My God!

For the past year, all I'd wanted was to hear these words. I would call him and beg him, every day, in the beginning. He would sit on the phone with me for hours and explain why the divorce was the best move for us. He would tell me why it had to be done. And then when I found out that Nada was pregnant, I gave up all hope for us ever getting back together again.

And now…

"I—I—"

"I know. It may sound crazy. But I'll do whatever I have to do to make you forgive me. Savannah, I'm sorry. I love you. And I know that you still love me too. If you don't want kids, fine. Okay. I'll live without them. As long as I don't have to live without you."

My heart fluttered.

I didn't know what to say.

"And no, you're not some second choice or option, just because she died. It's not like that. I don't want you to think that it is. The situation just really caused me to take a step back and think. It helped me to see the mistake I made. It helped me to see how wrong I was for leaving you. I was selfish. Forgive me."

Still, I didn't say anything.

"I have a celebrity surgery that I have to get back to do. I have to leave tonight. But I'll be back. I'll come here every week if I have to. Until you come back to me."

Nathaniel walked closer to me. I stood there frozen, speechless, as he kissed me on the cheek.

"That was Jace, wasn't it? Your first love? At the house?"

I'd told him stories about Jace when we first met.

I managed to nod.

"He may have been the first love. But I'll fight him and anyone else, to make sure that I'm your last. Come home Savannah. Come home to me."

Nathaniel smiled at me, and then he walked away from me without giving me a chance to respond. He got into his rental car, and with me still standing there, he drove away.

Wow!

Had I known that's what he was going to say, I would've gone home to talk to him a long time ago!

After standing there for a while, finally I forced my feet to move, and I walked to my car and hurried inside.

And then I just sat there. Staring at the hotel, trying to sort out my feelings.

I loved Nathaniel.

No. I *love* Nathaniel.

Still.

I think.

Ugh!

I'm not sure what I feel anymore.

And Jace.

Some old feelings for him have started to resurface. I was having a good time with him. And being around him, and with him, things were just…easy.

Even after Nathaniel popped up at the house yesterday, once he was gone, Jace never said a word about it. He didn't ask me any questions. He didn't act weird for the rest of the evening or anything. We actually had a pretty good time. And once I walked him out to leave, after he told me goodnight, he kissed me.

And it was even better than our first kiss. It was magical.

But Jace and I couldn't really have a future. Life for Jace was here. And I couldn't stay here. Not even for him.

And as for Nathaniel…

I started up my car and prepared to drive off with a head full of questions and a confused heart, but suddenly, I noticed her walking out of the hotel.

Marlo.

Wait a minute. What in the…

She wasn't alone. Cassy's husband, Corbin, walked close behind her. I coached myself not to jump to any conclusions, but I didn't have to.

Marlo smiled at him...just before he kissed her.

Damn it, Marlo!

He's your cousin's husband!

My heart started to race as I watched them flirt with each other and then finally, they let go of each other's hand.

Damn, I don't want to be here when this shit hits the fan!

They walked in separate directions, continuously looking back at each other.

I waited until both of them drove away, and then I drove like a bat out of hell towards grandma's house.

"What in the hell wrong witchu' girl?" Grandma placed her hands on her hips. Until that very moment, I hadn't noticed that I was panting. I took a seat on the couch next to her.

"Nothing."

"Um huh." She eyed me suspiciously.

Marlo. Marlo. Marlo!

I thought she had changed!

"And don't think you getting' on that road at all this week. You not goin' nowhere," grandma interrupted my thoughts.

I looked at her confused.

It was Monday.

And though I'd told Jace that I would stay until Friday for our date, after what Nathaniel just said to me and after what I just saw at the hotel, I was planning to break my commitment and leave out a little sooner.

"There's a hurricane headed our way," Grandma nodded towards the T.V. "It's supposed to hit us. The entire East coast. And I don't want you out there drivin' on that road in all of that mess. You're stayin' right here. And don't give me any lip."

I huffed.

The news said that the hurricane was expected to make landfall as early as Wednesday, and it was estimated to be as strong as a category three or four hurricane.

"We 'gots' to start preparing this house," Grandma said. "Everyone will probably come over here like they always do. Gonna' cook a good bit of food and stash some water, but we'll be fine. We always are. So…" she started. "Yo' ex-husband came here to get you, didn't he?" She changed the subject.

I smiled at her.

"Yeah, I knew that he hadn't come all this way for nothin'. He wants you back. For what it's worth, he seems like a nice man…but I think that you and Jayceon are cookin' up a little somethin'. I saw that kiss."

"And how did you see that grandma?"

"What you mean *how*? I stood right there in the damn window and watched. That's how," She chuckled. "That boy never quite got over you. I remember seeing him with that little wife of his. She was just an off-brand version of you. He'd married a woman that reminded him of you. Girl, she looks just like you. Sort of."

I hadn't seen any pictures of his wife, but I found grandma's comments interesting.

"Maybe you're here for a bigger reason. Other than just writing that little book of yours. I'm tellin' you, fate…destiny is a funny little thing," she smiled. "Are you goin' to the barbershop? Word 'round here is that Jayceon just bought the barbershop from Harvey and that there's goin' to be a little celebration there tonight."

I looked straight ahead, without blinking at the mention of Harvey's name. "No."

"Why not?"

"Just no Grandma."

I could feel her staring at me, but I refused to look at her.

"Well, okay then." Grandma stood up. "I want you to help me get Gamma's room cleaned out. There's no point in leavin' all of her stuff in there. She's passed on. Unlike you, she can't just pop up for a visit someday."

I nodded at her, just as my cell phone chimed.

Speaking of Jace.

"Hello."

"Hello, beautiful."

I smiled.

"Hey."

"So, it's official. I just bought the barbershop."

"Congratulations!"

"Thanks. We're having a little something here later. I want you to come."

There was no way in hell that I was going there. Harvey would be there. For years, Harvey had been there. I would never step foot in that place.

"Uh…I'm sorry Jace. Grandma wants me to help her pack up Gamma's old room tonight. I can't make it."

I looked up to see grandma staring at me in curiosity. It was as though she was thinking, wondering, what the real reason behind me not wanting to go to the barbershop was.

"Oh. I completely understand. I need to see you. I don't think I can wait until Friday. So, when can I see you?"

"I don't know."

"Tomorrow I'll be busy doing some things at the shop, but what about Wednesday?"

"A hurricane is coming on Wednesday."

"Shit. That's what they always say. Can I pick you up around 5?"

"Is this going to be considered as our little date?" I giggled.

"If you want it to be."

"Okay."

"Okay," he copied me. "I'll holla' at you later on."

We hung up.

"There's somethin' in the water that ain't clean," Grandma said. That was an old saying that meant that something just didn't seem right. "Is there somethin' that you aren't telling me?" Grandma asked.

"Nope. So, what do you need me to do first?"

I stood up.

For a while, grandma continued to stare at me, and then finally she turned around and headed down the hall. I followed behind her, and just as I exhaled she said, "I'm gonna' find out what it is Vana. Watch and see. I'm gonna' find out what you're not telling me."

Umph.

She'll never get my secret out of me.

~***~

"You look just like your mother."

A chill slithered down my spine.

I recognized his voice without turning around.

Harvey.

The town was going crazy.

It was complete chaos, everywhere, as folks tried to grab last minute things for the hurricane. Grandma Whinny sent me to the grocery store for a few things, and although I barely got half of the stuff on her list, it had taken me over an hour and a half just to make it through the checkout line.

"Let me help you---"

"I got it!" I shouted without looking behind me. I hurriedly unloaded the cart, literally throwing the groceries inside my trunk.

I felt as though I was going to be sick.

"Aw, don't act like that now. Uncle Harvey…"

"You're not my goddamn uncle!" I growled as I slammed the trunk closed. And then…

I turned around to face him.

I faced the man that had violated me. The man that had stolen my sanity for so many years. The man that had hurt me, and for a long time made me feel unworthy.

Finally, I faced the enemy.

Harvey stared at me. He looked as though he was only days away from death.

God don't like ugly.

And what an ugly sight he was.

He wasn't the stocky, polished man that he was back then. Now, he was skinny, with dark patches all over his skin.

"Damn. You're feisty just like your mama was too. Um, um, um you're all grown up now."

He looked at me as though I was a piece of meat. His grin was sinful. It was the same smile that he'd worn on his face that night.

I didn't respond to him. Truthfully, I felt as though I was going to faint, but I didn't show it. I didn't want him to think that he had that much power on me. I wouldn't give him the satisfaction. Remaining silent, I pushed the cart out of my way, and then I reached for my car door.

Harvey grabbed ahold of my shirt.

"Don't you dare fucking touch me! Don't ever put your goddamn hands on me again!" I yelled at the top of my lungs, causing everyone to stop and stare.

Harvey raised his hands in the air with a smile.

"Ay, calm down, little lady. You're mad at the wrong person."

"The wrong person? I'm mad at the wrong person?" I asked him comically. "Oh no, you're the right fucking person! And I hope you burn in hell for what you did to me!" The last part I somewhat whispered so no one could hear me.

After all of these years, I was still ashamed.

Harvey chuckled. "Have you ever asked yourself why you were there in the first place? Ever wondered why you ended up at the house?"

What?

I didn't bother asking him for an explanation. Instead, I got into my car, and hurriedly, I put my car in reverse. Harvey just stood there, as though he wasn't going to move, so I started to back up.

He slammed his hands against the roof of my car.

"Hey!" He shouted.

"Then get the fuck out of my way!" I growled just as I put my car into drive and sped away. I kept glancing back at him in my rearview mirror until he was out of sight.

Once I couldn't see him anymore, I rolled down the windows, and let out a scream.

"Ahhh!"

My heart was pounding. Every inch of my body was shaking, especially my hands. I was struggling to catch my breath, and the wind seemed to make things worse, so I rolled the windows back up. I pulled over onto the side of the road.

I hadn't known what I would do or say if I ever saw him again. I was hoping that I never would.

I started to cry for so many reasons. For what seemed like a million little things. I felt afraid, but I didn't want to be. I knew that I didn't have to be, but I did.

I bawled uncontrollably, for what seemed like forever, and then I forced myself to get back on the road. I allowed the tears to fall up until I turned onto the dirt road that would lead to the plantation house. And then I wiped my face. I told myself that I was okay.

And then I remembered Harvey's words.

Why did I end up there that night?

What had he meant by that?

I couldn't drive but so far down the gravel driveway because of all the cars. I took a shortcut through the grass to get as close as I could to the house.

It was Wednesday, and already, it was windy.

It definitely felt as though a hurricane was on its way. They weren't expecting it to make landfall until sometime that night, but most of my family was already off of work and already at the house, prepared to face the storm together.

Strangely, I wanted to be somewhere else.

I just wanted to be alone.

My breathing steadied, just as a couple of raindrops hit my windshield. My phone buzzed, and I read Nathaniel's text messages as they came in. He asked how the weather was, and if I was going to be okay. And then he asked me if I was ignoring him.

I wasn't.

I just didn't really know what to say him. To calm him down, I replied to him and told him that nothing was happening as of yet and that I would call him later. And then I just sat there.

Lost in my thoughts.

Wishing that I could go home.

I saw Marlo, Cassy, and Tatiana come out of the house and walk down the porch steps. Marlo led them as they headed in my direction.

Grandma had probably been looking out the window and instructed them to come and help me with the bags, once she noticed that I wasn't getting out of the car.

Marlo.

Cassy.

I replayed the images of seeing Marlo and Cassy's husband Corbin, kissing and holding hands. I didn't plan on saying anything about what I saw. I kept telling myself that it wasn't any of my business. And it wasn't.

All I had to do was mind my business.

Marlo knocked on my driver's side window.

I reached down by my knee to pop the trunk, and then I opened the door.

"Hey girl," Marlo said. The others said hey as well.

"Hey. The stuff is in the trunk."

"What's wrong with you?"

"Nothing. I'm just tired."

Marlo stared at me as though she didn't believe me.

We all grabbed a bag or two, and then we chatted as we walked towards the house.

"Hey, really, what's wrong?" Marlo whispered to me as the other ladies walked ahead.

"I saw him."

"Saw who?"

"Harvey."

She stopped walking at the mention of his name. I looked at her. "And I saw you and Corbin too." I turned away from her, without giving her a chance to respond.

Damn it, Savannah! You talk too much!

I entered the noisy house, and one of the men immediately took the bags out of my hand. It was so hot and stuffy, and there were people in every direction. Talking and laughing with one another. Grandma was right in the center of it all, smiling as though she was her happiest when a lot family was around. I saw Marlo trying to get to me through the crowd, but I kept walking further and further away from her.

I made my way through the kitchen, and then I hurried out the door onto the back porch. The rain was falling lightly now, but still, I headed to take a seat on the edge of the porch.

"Hey," I heard him say, just as I sat down.

Jace.

"Hey."

"I knocked on the front door, but nobody answered."

"It's a lot of people in there, they probably didn't hear it."

"I figured. That's why I came around back."

"You could've called me."

"I did."

I looked for my phone, and then I realized that I'd left it in my car.

"You ready to go?"

"What?"

"It's Wednesday."

I chuckled. "In case you haven't notice, a hurricane really is coming."

"We better get going then, so that I can cook for you. Just in case the power goes out."

"Really?"

"Yes. Really. You'll be safe with me, V. I'll never let anything happen to you. Besides, it wouldn't be so bad if we got stuck inside together, for a few days, would it?" He smiled.

I couldn't help but grin.

"Jace, what are you up to?"

"Nothing V. I just want to spend some time with you before you leave. You know just in case it's another fifteen years before I see you again."

I wasn't in the mood, but I didn't know how to tell him that. I didn't want to hurt his feelings. Seeing Harvey had thrown me off. I could barely think straight.

"I mean would you rather be stuck in the house with me? Or with all of them?" Jace asked. He laughed once I jumped to my feet.

"Good point. Let's go."

Marlo came out onto the back porch, just as I took Jace's hand.

"I'll be back."

She nodded at me, and then I followed Jace to his truck.

He opened the door and helped me inside.

It was a nice truck. Big. Black. The kind that he'd always said that he wanted, just a newer model of course. It had big chrome rims, and it fit him a lot better than the Mercedes SUV that he also had.

Jace got into the truck, and I watched him as he started to back up.

"So, what are you cooking?"

"It's a surprise."

"Cheap date."

He laughed.

"Ain't nothing cheap about me baby," he said as he picked up the remote that controlled the radio.

I made myself comfortable as he found a song and tuned it up.

"What you know about that?" He glanced back and forth between me and the road.

"This used to be your song," I grinned at him. Jace started to mumble through the words of the song until it got to the chorus.

"Candy rain!"

Jace sung at the top of his lungs and with both hands on the wheel, he attempted to do an old dance that we called "The Snake".

I laughed at him from a good healthy place.

"Come on, what you got?" He joked as I reached for the remote.

"Don't ever sing in front of anyone else again."

"Aw, come on. I sounded good. Don't *hate* on my vocals."

"Trust me. I'm not. You sounded like a hit dog," I insulted him as I clicked through the songs. "Oh. Okay. See this is what I'm talking about."

I turned up the song.

"Okay. Okay. I can get with that. Let me see what you got."

Using the remote as a microphone, I sang: *"This is how we do it!"*

Jace and I used to love Montell Jordan. It didn't take long for Jace to join in. We laughed, somewhat danced and mumbled our way through the song and in unison we kept screaming *'this is how we do it!'* whenever it came time to say those words.

And for the rest of the car ride song after song, we relived the 80's and 90's until finally, we came to a stop.

"I need that playlist," I smiled at him.

"I got you."

I reached to open the truck's door.

"You better not open that door. I got it," Jace said.

I grinned.

A true Southern Gentleman.

I waited on Jace to walk around the truck and open my door. I observed the one level home in front of me. I hadn't been to Mount Holly, the town where Jace lived since I was a little girl, but the city had come a mighty long way.

Jace lived in a subdivision.

Considering the weather, no one was outside, but it seemed like a quiet place to live.

Jace's house was an off-white color, with a hunter green trim. I'll admit, the house looked a little on the feminine side with the porch decorations, the landscape and even the wreath on the front door. I couldn't help but wonder if it was the home that he and his ex-wife had once shared.

"Don't just stand there. Come on, before your wig *fly* off."

"What? This is all my hair, thank you!"

"Sure it is," Jace laughed, and led the way.

"Your landscaper must be a woman."

"She is. My ex-wife," he said as he opened his front door. "She and her family own a landscaping company. Once we divorced, she decided to move, so I kept the house. The outside is all her doing, but the inside," Jace turned on the lights. "The inside is all me."

There was leather everywhere. And big, flat screen T.V.s. One in the living room, and one in the kitchen. I smiled at how clean it was.

"Well, it's cleaner than I thought it would be," I commented.

"Oh, you got jokes, huh?"

We both chuckled.

"Follow me."

He locked the front door, and then I followed him down a short narrow hallway, and into what appeared to be the master bedroom.

"Your Grandma helped me with your sizes."

Jace glanced at the black dress that was lying on his bed.

"It's beautiful," I beamed.

He started to point at all of the other items that he'd gotten me and told me that I could use his bathroom to freshen up.

"And this "date" begins," Jace said, and then he left the room, closing the door behind him.

I held the dress close to my chest as I examined the rhinestones on the shoes that he'd picked out to go with it.

I was impressed, to say the least.

Jace had even picked out the perfect bra and panty set, and it was just the right size.

Grandma's nosey ass.

I admired the red and black color scheme throughout his bedroom. It was mostly black with different framed Scarface Posters giving the room small pops of red.

I found it hilarious and sweet that Jace thought to pick up body wash, and it was my favorite scent from back when we were in high school.

Cucumber Melon.

I headed into the bathroom, where I saw that he already had a towel and washcloth waiting for me.

Wow!

I was stunned.

He really thought this night through.

I couldn't get out of my damp clothes fast enough to shower and slip on the dress. The plunging neckline was to die for, and I loved the way that it hugged my hips. I wished that I had brought my make-up bag. I'd left with nothing. No purse. No cellphone. Nothing; except for my car keys.

Jace had me all to himself.

After teasing my curls and slipping on the shoes that Jace had purchased to compliment the dress, I opened the bedroom door and followed the sound of music.

I found Jace in the kitchen.

He towered over the stove.

I noticed that he had changed his clothes too. I figured that he must've gotten dressed in another bathroom or bedroom. I could only see the back of him, but he was wearing a pair of black casual pants and a red collared shirt.

I shifted my focus from him to the layout of his home. I admired the open floor concept of his house. I loved being able to see the living room, and the kitchen at the same time. I wished that my home in New York had been made that way.

Jace had the blinds open, and with him still unaware that I was in the room, I walked towards the window.

It was raining cats and dogs now, and the branches of the trees were swaying forcefully as a result of the wind.

It's coming.

And instead of watching the news and being worried about the hurricane; like normal folks do, this man was consumed with cooking for me and determined to show me a good time.

"Emotions make you cry sometimes…"

Jace sang as he turned around and noticed me standing there. He smiled as he wiped his hands on the black and white apron that he was wearing on top of his clothes.

I grinned at him, immaturely, as he reached out his hand. I walked towards him, and as soon as I was close enough, I grabbed his hand.

"Absolutely beautiful," he said.

"Thank you. I see you cleaned up yourself too. I guess you look okay."

"Oh, just okay. Dang. What does a man gotta' do to get a compliment from you?" He smiled. I knew that he was joking, but internally, I told myself to stop giving him such a hard time.

The cologne that he was wearing smelled so good that I closed my eyes as I inhaled. Jace released my hand and pulled out a chair from the table. For the first time, I noticed that it was set.

Fresh, long-stemmed roses were in the center of the table in a crystal vase. There were two vanilla colored candles on each side of it. Their small flames danced as though they were gyrating to an unheard tune.

There were two bottles of wine in front of me.

One red. One white.

Two nice sized wine glasses and two rectangle plates with silverware placed neatly on top of black and gold cloth napkins.

"You really thought this through, didn't you?"

"Yes. Just for you."

Once I sat down, Jace scooted me closer to the table, and then he picked up my wine glass. "Red or White?"

"Red."

I watched him as he poured the wine.

"Thank you."

"No problem. Your food is almost done."

"I didn't know you could cook."

"How would you know?"

There was a moment of awkward silence.

"Well, it smells good. What is it?"

"My famous shrimp and broccoli alfredo, a fresh salad with the works and homemade lobster biscuits."

"Oh, so you can *cook-cook*?" I teased him.

"So, you just gonna' say it twice like that?" He chuckled. "Then yes, I guess I can *cook-cook*. As you say. I thought you said you used to be an editor."

I stuck up my middle finger at him.

Jace shook his head and headed back to the stove.

In admiration, I watched him as I took a sip of my wine.

Briefly, I wondered what life would've been like if I'd stayed around. I was sure that we would've gotten married. Yeah. Of course, we would've. I was sure that we would've had a house full of kids by now. I wondered if he would've actually made it to the league, and I wondered if I would've ever pursued my goals and dreams, or if my whole life would've been about making him happy.

There's no doubt in my mind that life would've been different. And I wondered if it would've been better.

Maybe.

Jace started to take off his apron. He hung it on a rack attached to the back of the pantry door, and then he picked up my plate.

We were both quiet.

It was as though neither of us knew what to say.

"Dinner is served."

He placed the plate in front of me.

I took a whiff and beamed.

"Wow. This looks good."

"I bet it tastes even better," he tooted his own horn.

"We'll see about that."

I picked up my fork as he picked up his plate and headed to the stove to pile it with food.

I closed my eyes as I savored the first bite of alfredo.

Umm.

"Good ain't it?"

Jace took his seat in the chair across from me.

"I can't even lie. It's so damn good."

"That's because I made it with love."

Love?

What is he trying to say?

"Relax, V. I didn't ask you to marry me," Jace picked up his fork after noticing my facial expression. "But yes, I still have love for you. And there ain't a damn thing that you can do about it."

Well, alright then.

The next hour or so could be best described as heaven on earth. Jace and I ate. We talked. Laughed. Sang to each other. He complimented me more times than I could count, and he was so transparent that it was refreshing. I didn't have to guess what he was feeling. He told me exactly what was on his mind. I was on his. And he was the only thing on mine. And here, with him, was the only place in the whole world that I wanted to be.

"Uh oh."

The lights flickered on and off.

"Things must be getting bad out there."

Jace put both of our plates into the sink, and I followed him towards the window with my wine glass in my hand.

Now, it was about eight o'clock in the evening.

We both just stood there.

Somewhat admiring the beautiful chaos through the darkness.

It was strange.

Bad weather and natural disasters usually scared me half to death, but for the first time ever, and though something so awful was coming, I felt safe. I felt at peace.

"Just in case things get bad, and you're stuck here with me for a few days, I went out and got everything that we could possibly need. I got plenty of everything."

Jace inched closer to me and started to caress my left hand.

My feelings were all over the place, but one emotion was crystal clear.

Desire.

"If I could turn back the hands of time I wouldn't have left you like that. I would've at least asked you to come with me."

"I would've."

"Really? You would've left behind everything and everyone for me?"

"With no questions asked."

My heart skipped a beat.

This is why I loved him so much back then.

Now I remember.

I placed my fingers in between his.

"How am I ever going to leave you behind again?"

Why did I just say that?

"You don't have to. Let me just put that shit out there."

Jace made an uncomfortable moment for me humorous, but before I could reply, it was as though the sky opened up and poured out so much rain that the house seemed to tremble. Instantly, the music that was playing in the background stopped, and the lights went out.

Jace let go of my hand and went to work lighting candles all over the place. He must've gone out and grabbed every candle that was left on the shelf.

"I have flashlights too, but I think all these damn candles should do it for now."

Jace headed back towards the window. The room glowed from the candlelight, as I took a seat on the big, black sectional that took up most of the living room. For a while, we didn't speak. It seemed as though we were both listening to what was going on outside.

"Is this seat taken?" Jace asked sarcastically, and then he sat down beside me. As soon as he was seated, he pulled me close to him.

"Big daddy gotta' protect you, so you gotta' sit *really* close okay?"

"Oh yeah? Okay."

I snuggled up against him but, apparently, he wanted to be even closer than he already was, so Jace pulled me onto his lap and somewhat cradled me in his arms as though I was a newborn child.

"Yeah. That's better."

The candlelight caused his skin to resemble 'melt in your mouth' caramel, and suddenly, I had this dying urge to lick him.

He stared at me.

I stared back at him.

"Looking in your eyes reminds me of the good ole' days. Me and you. All the memories. I was ten on the day that I looked at you during church and thought: Savannah will be my wife. A little young to be worried about marriage, but I've always had this feeling that it was gonna' be you. That it was supposed to be you."

He used his left hand to place my curls behind my ear.

I opened my mouth to say something, but hurriedly, I clamped it shut. I decided to admire him, silently, instead. I allowed myself to remember the feelings that I'd had for him, back in the day. I remembered all the good times that we'd shared. I remembered how he used to make me feel. And most of all, I remembered that he was supposed to be my forever.

"If you had one wish, what would it be?" I finally managed to say.

For only a second, Jace appeared to be thinking about the question. And then, he said: "If I had one wish, right now, it would be..." He paused, smiled, and then proceeded. "My wish would be you. All of you. Everything about you. To have you. To know you. To love you. Just you."

I beamed at him, and then without talking myself out of it, I kissed him. I kissed him slowly, with a lot of passion, and a little bit of everything else. I apologized to him with my mouth for walking away from him, and for not taking him with me.

Jace's hands roamed all over my body, and I felt as though I was melting from his touch. He caressed me, he hugged me, he squeezed me, all while never taking his lips off mine.

My heart was racing, and my body temperature started to rise. I was so turned on that my clit thumped with anticipation and pleaded for an opportunity to explode.

I wanted him.

And I was going to have him.

All of a sudden, I started to wonder what would happen afterward.

How would I feel?

How hard would it be for me to leave?

I knew that I couldn't stay here, and I knew that Jace couldn't go with me. His business was here. His daughter was here. His life was here. And my life was in New York.

Sex would just make it harder to say goodbye.

I pulled away from him.

I noticed the thickness of his *wood* for the first time, and longing to feel *it* inside me, I was tempted to kiss him again, but I didn't.

Instead, I got up from his lap.

"Um...um...I'm thirsty."

I could see the confused look on his face as I turned away from him. I rushed into the kitchen. I grabbed the bottle of wine from the table and drank from it.

No. No more alcohol.

I was already horny, and alcohol was just going to make it worse. After sitting down the bottle, I walked over to the kitchen sink and turned on the faucet.

"I need a cup," I mumbled, as I started to open and shut the kitchen cabinets. I'd heard Jace get up, but I didn't turn around. I found a glass and filled it up with water. I stood close to the sink, slowly drinking the water and trying to gather my thoughts.

I could hear Jace moving things around behind me, but I didn't know what he was doing. All I knew was that this night with him had been perfect. I knew that talking to him and being around him made me feel things that I hadn't felt in years.

I knew...

Jace touched me from behind, and I jumped slightly.

He reached around me and turned off the faucet. He took the glass out of my hand and placed it into the sink. And then he turned me around to face him.

He touched the sides of my face with his big hands, and I closed my eyes. I listened to the rain as it slammed against the windows and the roof. I listened to the rumbling wind. And then I listened to my heart.

I opened my eyes.

Without saying a word, Jace pulled me toward the kitchen table. I saw that he'd taken the vase, the wine, and the candles off of it and placed them along the small bar.

Jace moved one of the chairs and still silent, he picked me up and sat me on the edge of the table.

I was nervous.

"You might not understand why or how but---I love you V. I always have. I always will."

I exhaled.

"I love you too."

Really Savannah?

Did you really love him?

I wasn't sure if I meant those words.

I feel something, but is it love?

It couldn't be? Could it? After all this time?

I was confused.

Jace leaned in to kiss me. I kissed him back knowing that we were going all the way this time. We kissed for a while, and then he laid me back on the table.

Jace ran his hands up the sides of my thighs, pushing my dress up until it was past my stomach. I found myself glancing at his shadow on the wall as I slightly lifted my hips so that he could remove my panties.

We were both panting.

I was sweating, and I started to hyperventilate once Jace spread my legs apart. He rubbed my clitoris with his thumb, and I closed my eyes. It had been so long since I'd had sex. Mentally, I coached my body to relax and enjoy the ride.

Gently, Jace continued to massage my *bean* and then I felt him slip a finger inside me to examine my wetness.

His finger moved around inside me momentarily, and then I heard a sucking noise once he pulled his finger out. I opened my eyes to look at him. Jace was sucking on his finger. The sight of him tasting my juices turned me all the way on, and I begged him with my eyes to taste me again.

With his nasty self!

Jace got down on his knees, and then he pulled me towards the edge of the kitchen table.

I waited.

I waited.

And then finally, his lips kissed the lips of my vagina, and then immediately afterward, I felt the warmth of his tongue. I bellowed with pleasure almost instantly. Within seconds, I became mesmerized by the way that his tongue moved. I whined, I cooed and gripped the sides of the wooden table as Jace attempted to *suck my soul* out of me.

This feeling.

This...this...feeling.

It was even better than I'd imagined it would be. Ten times better than it had been when we were teens.

Yes! Oh yes!

I felt as though I was about to explode. I was right there. The best orgasm of my life was right there, until...he stopped.

Wait...no, no, no!

Keep going!

My eyes popped open, and I saw Jace standing to his feet. Immediately, he sat me up and pulled the dress over my head. He took off my bra and then hurriedly, he undressed. Naked, he picked me up from the table and then placed me onto the kitchen floor. The floor was cold and caused me to arch my back, but the minute Jace put my left breast in his mouth, I forgot about the chill and focused on what he was doing to my nipple.

I was dripping wet, and I felt my juices seeping to the area in between my thighs. Jace moved from one breast to the other and then he started to kiss me everywhere in between. Finally, once I was all fore-played out, he positioned himself just right in between my legs.

The candlelight.

The rain.

The sound of the wind.

The moment...that moment was perfect. And, it became even better as soon as Jace entered my most sacred *dominion*.

Jace and I rocked back and forth on the kitchen floor for innumerable minutes. He explored the deepest parts of me. He took me to sexual heights that I'd never explored.

Sex had never meant so much to me before. It was close. It was intimate. It was perfect. It was intense. We looked into each other's eyes with every stroke. We kissed with every moan. We connected on an undiscovered level.

135

We…yes…we made love.

"Good morning."

I opened my eyes to look at Jace.

Last night was like a dream.

After having sex on the kitchen floor, we made our way into the living room where we made love again on his sectional and then again on the living room floor.

"Hi," I smiled at him.

Jace kissed me.

"Last night…" I started.

"Yeah. I know," Jace agreed without me having to say anything else. "The phones aren't working. The cell towers must be down."

I didn't care about anything. I was still high off him.

"I wonder how it looks outside."

Jace got up, and I appreciated his massive, naked frame as he walked towards the window.

"Damn. It's fucked up out here. From what I can see, trees are down. And street signs are too. And it's a good bit of water, and still raining. The roads are probably bad. Looks like you're going to be stuck here with me for a few days," Jace grinned as though he was up to something.

"Okay," I smiled back.

I got off the floor to go take a look out the window, just to see if he was exaggerating.

He wasn't.

It was a mess outside.

We'd heard it all last night, but we were too busy exploring each other. Instinctively, I wondered how it was back at the house with my family. They were in the country parts, so I was sure that things were probably flooded and even worse, but it wasn't like I could call them to check on them.

Funny. I was worried about them. I cared. Back in New York, even during times like this, I would barely think twice about them.

Being here was changing me.

Or maybe it was reminding me of who I used to be.

"I don't know how long the power is gonna' be out, but I do have a radio in the garage. I'm going to go get it, and we can listen in and see if anything is being said."

I nodded at Jace.

He disappeared for a moment, and then he came back with his gym shorts on. He opened a side door, which I assumed went out into the garage, and then he closed the door behind him.

Naked, I got up and flopped down on the couch with a smile.

Oh My God!

I couldn't stop smiling.

I hadn't planned on any of this. I hadn't planned on seeing Jace, and I definitely hadn't planned on having sex with him.

This cannot be happening!

Still grinning, the doorbell rang. I looked towards the door, wondering why Jace was at the front door, instead of coming back through the side door.

I hurried to open it.

I didn't even try to cover up my nakedness as I turned the knob. I opened the door.

"Oh my god!"

I covered my body once I noticed that it was a woman.

She was wearing rain boots and a raincoat, and she looked at me confused.

I kept one arm over my chest and one hand covering my private area as she took off her hood.

Wow.

It was like looking into a mirror.

It was as though she was my twin.

If what grandma had told me about her was true, this had to be Jace's ex-wife. This had to be Reeva.

Damn! She really does look like me!

"Um...I thought you were..." I was embarrassed. "You must be Jace's ex-wife."

"Ex-wife? Who told you that? Last time I checked...Jace and I are *still* married."

My mouth dropped open.

What?

****

CHAPTER FIVE

I think I'm in love.

"These past four days..."

"Felt like forever," I completed his sentence.

I was stuck at Jace's house for four days as a result of the hurricane. And each day, I fell more and more in love with him all over again.

Reeva showed up on day one.

Jace hadn't mentioned that she lived only two houses down from him. He'd come back in through the side door to find me standing there in my *birthday suit*, and her standing in front of me.

I was in shock by what she'd said about still being his wife, but as it turns out, she was just been being an ass about the details.

She *is* his ex-wife.

They haven't been together in over two years, but it wasn't until recently that they'd signed the divorce papers. They were still waiting on the finalized divorce documents to come in the mail, but Reeva was in fact, no longer Jace's wife.

Bitch.

Jace asked her what she wanted and where his daughter was, as I backed away from them. I rushed to his bedroom, but I continued to listen to their conversation.

Reeva ignored his questions, at first, and instead, she talked about me. She commented on how much we look alike. She accused Jace of only pursuing her because of our resemblance. She knows who I am. I was surprised. She called me his 'first love that he never stopped loving'. She said that she'd always had to work a little bit harder to make him love her more than he'd loved me. She seemed disappointed that after all these years, somehow, he'd found his way back to me.

Jace told her to mind her business, and then he asked her again where their daughter was and why she'd come by. He told her that he'd planned on walking over to check on them. She told him that their daughter was okay and that she'd been asking for her tablet; which she'd left in her room at Jace's house.

Jace went to get it, after explaining to her that it may not be charged, since the power was out.

I found a long shirt and a pair of shorts in Jace's drawer. I put the pieces of clothing on, just as they started to speak again.

Jace told her that the tablet was dead, and she asked him if I'd moved back to town.

Jace said no.

I came out of his room. Jace told me that he was going to walk Reeva home, see his daughter and that he would be right back. His ex-wife didn't say anything else to me, though I did spot the big, diamond ring on her finger. She'd cut her eyes at me, just as Jace led her out the front door, and closed the door behind them.

Thirty-minutes later, Jace came back and explained everything.

After explaining their status to me, Jace told me that the day after they signed their divorce papers, the guy she's been seeing proposed to her. He actually lived with her, and Jace's daughter. Jace said that they got along pretty well.

He didn't want Reeva. Reeva didn't want him. Jace made sure that I understood that. So, other than that little run-in with *my twin*, the rest of the time with Jace was basically amazing.

We had so much sex that I could barely walk. We wrestled, ran around the house like kids, danced and played hide and seek. Jace grilled food for us because until the fourth day, we didn't have any power. He rubbed my feet. Boiled pots of water on the grill so that I could have a warm bath. At night, we would talk until the sun came up, and every night, I fell asleep in his arms.

What we shared was beautiful.

Needless to say, I was sad that our time together had come to an end. Jace had to check on the barbershop, so he was dropping me off at the plantation house. He drove as far down the gravel driveway as he could.

"Damn," Jace commented as I looked around.

Three huge trees had fallen down in the yard. The one that had the tire swing attached to it had been pulled up from the roots and had fallen on top of my cousin Roxanne's car. The yard was a mess, and the house had taken a beaten too. Shingles and shutters had been blown away. Clover had been hit a lot worse than the town that Jace lived in.

"I love you," Jace said.

I looked at him in the eyes before I responded. "I love you too." And I meant it. I hadn't been sure a few days ago, but I was now. I'd fallen in love with my first love---again.

We shared a kiss, and then I got out of his truck wearing another pair of his gym shorts and a shirt.

I inspected my car.

The windshield was cracked from a big branch that had been thrown against it, but other than that and a few other scratches it was okay.

The yard was still full of cars, but not as many as it had been before. And as I reached the front porch, I noticed that the porch steps were pretty much gone...literally. Pieces of wood were missing from them, and I had to jump onto the porch to get to the front door.

I was hoping that their power was back on, and even if it wasn't, I was sure that there was a generator or two somewhere around. Grandma liked to be prepared.

I walked inside.

It wasn't as loud as I expected it to be.

I heard lots of noise above my head and figured that it was probably the children running around.

Only Uncle Willie and two of my cousin's husbands were in the living room, and I made my way towards the kitchen.

"Wow, I almost forgot that you were *here*," Cassy smirked.

Bitch, your husband almost forgot that you were his wife.

I didn't say my thoughts out loud.

"Well, well, well, I'm glad to see that you are safe," grandma said.

I noticed that the women were trying to put something together for everyone to eat.

"How bad was it where you were?"

"It didn't hit Mount Holly as bad as it hit here. But the roads were bad; I couldn't get back."

"Just glad you're okay. We all made it through it. Thankfully. I helped Jayceon get everythin' ready for you. Did you like it?"

"Yes, ma'am. I did."

"Well, I want details! All of the dirty ones! So, spill it! What happened with you and Jace? Did y'all 'do it'?" Tatiana smiled.

I noticed that Marlo wasn't there. And Corbin wasn't there either.

"We had a good time," I said, coyly.

"Did you let him *hit it* or what? Chile, you better had let him *hit* that! Lord knows I would've!" Eve screamed.

"Shit, I would've too," Cassy shrugged.

Grandma seemed to be waiting for my answer too.

"Y'all are so nosey," I laughed, refusing to answer their questions.

I excused myself to go put on some clothes that fit. The room that I slept in was still intact. As though no one had been in there. Remembering that my phone, as well as my purse, were still inside my car, I changed my clothes and then headed back outside.

I observed my window again, and then I unlocked my car doors and got inside. My purse was still on the floor, and my phone was in the seat. It was dead, so I turned on my car and connected it to my car charger. After a few minutes, it turned on.

I had so many missed calls, voicemails, and text messages from Nathaniel that started to come through.

Nathaniel.

I hadn't thought about him in days.

I hadn't thought about what he'd said to me, and after spending the last few days with Jace, I couldn't really be sure if what he'd said still mattered.

I sent him a quick text message and told him that I was okay and that the town had lost power. I told him that I would call him soon, and that I was sorry if I caused him to worry.

I also had a few other messages and calls from friends back home. Grandma had called me twice, on the first night of the storm and I also had one call, and a text message from Marlo from that day.

She said that we needed to talk.

My phone vibrated in my hand.

Seeing that it was Jace, I smiled; until I read his message.

Jace said that he was at the barbershop and that it was in pretty bad shape. I told him that everything was going to be okay and I asked him to call me when he could.

I waited for a while to see if Nathaniel was going to text me back, but he didn't. So, I found my insurance information and called in about my window.

After finally getting a representative on the line and filing a claim, finally, I headed back inside the house.

"Grandma was looking for you," Tatiana said.

I headed towards her bedroom.

"Grand---"

She froze, and so did I, once I opened her door.

She waited for me to say something and when I didn't, she continued to put the wrap that was in her hands, back over her bald head. Her hair used to be long and beautiful, but now it was all gone.

"Cancer."

My heart stopped beating for only a second.

"I had cancer. It's gone now. I beat it. I rang the bell just the other week. A few days before you popped up to be exact."

"You...you...had cancer?"

"Yes. And no one but the people that were living in this house knew about it. Gamma and Willie. I fought the fight for almost two years. I didn't need nobody feelin' sorry for me. I couldn't slow down. I had too much to do. Too many people to take care of. Too many folks depend on me. But I made it. I had a surgery, got my treatments, and I beat it. It's goin' take a lot more than some damn cancer to take me out."

I was stuck.

I didn't know whether to hug her or to smile.

"My hair will grow back. I'm gonna' be just fine."

"How could you keep something like that a secret? Weren't you sick?"

"Sometimes, but I managed. The doctors caught it early. The few that knew I had to have surgery, thought that it was for something else. I did what I had to do. And now it's gone. At least for now. And hopefully forever. I didn't see any reason to worry folks. There was no point in tellin' my whole family. It's my business. And I would like to keep it that way."

I nodded.

"Anyway, I need you to do me a favor again. I need you to see if you can make it across town to check on Livy. I went by there just before things got bad, but she wasn't there. I was gonna' get her to come over here. I know yo' windshield cracked, but you can drive my car. Can you go check on her, please? If the roads are clear that way?"

"Jace made it to the barbershop, so the roads should be fine. I'll go."

Thinking about Livy caused me to remember my run-in with Harvey. And thinking of him, made me remember what he'd said about the real reason I'd ended up at their house on prom night.

I could ask Livy what he meant by that.

I ended up driving Tatiana's car since hers was the easiest to get out, and still intact. I drove cautiously to the other side of town. There were orange signs signaling road closures all over the place. Abandoned cars. Trees had fallen down all over the place. Buildings and businesses had been destroyed.

Speaking of...

Slowly, I drove by the barbershop.

Oh no.

It was ruined!

A light pole had fallen through the window of the barbershop and half of the roof was missing.

Literally! And that's just from what I could see.

Jace and a few others were standing outside.

I couldn't imagine how he felt. The ink was barely dry on the paperwork, and now the barbershop was destroyed.

Thankfully, the little road to Livy's house was clear. Her yard was a mess, but there weren't any trees down or anything, so hopefully she was okay.

I knocked on the door.

"Livy?"

She opened it.

"You're still here."

She walked away from the door after inviting me inside.

The house was clean, and so was she. She didn't appear to be high. *Good.*

"Grandma just wanted me to come over and check on you."

"I'm fine," she said as she took a seat on the old couch. "The last time you were here. The things I said...I remembered once I was..."

"Look. Your secrets are safe with me. And actually, there's something that I wanted to ask you about."

Nerves tried to intimidate me.

I wasn't sure about mentioning what Harvey had done to me to her, but I knew that telling her my secret was the only way to ask her about the comment that he'd made.

"It happened to me too."

She looked at me as though she was waiting for me to proceed.

"Uh...what Harvey did to you...it happened to me too."

Livy jumped up to her feet so fast that it caught me off guard. She started to pace back and forth.

"Harvey raped me," I said aloud.

Breathe, Savannah. Just breathe.

"He raped me on prom night. He was part of the reason why I went away. And then he told me if I told anyone, I was going to end up dead. Just like my mother."

Livy's bottom lip started to tremble, and she sat back down.

"I haven't really told anyone about what happened to me that night. I'm telling you now because you told me. And because I ran into Harvey and he said something that I didn't understand. He asked me if I knew why I ended up at your house that night. What does that mean? Do you know?"

A single tear fell from Livy's right eye.

"What did he mean Livy?'

She opened her mouth and then she clamped it shut. She closed her eyes and then finally, she muttered her next words.

"He asked me *for* you."

What?

"Excuse me?"

I could see the regret all over her face.

"He asked me for you."

"He asked you *for* me?"

"Yes."

I started to back away from her.

"What do you mean he *asked* you for me?"

Livy stood up.

"He asked me to get you to stay over after the prom. So...so...so he could do to you what he'd been doing to me."

"What!"

No! No! No!

I couldn't have heard her right. I started to shake my head.

"Harvey had been obsessed with your mama. My mother knew it too. She would always fuss at him about the way she would catch him looking at her. One night, I heard them arguing about rumors of him coming on to your mama at the bar on Peach Street. He told mama that nothing happened. And that your mama turned him down and threw a drink in his face."

I felt as though I was about to have a heart attack.

Had Harvey killed my mother?

"All I know is that he'd wanted her, but he couldn't have her. And then she died. And then on the night of the prom, he asked me for you."

Livy started to cry, hard.

"He told me that if I didn't get you to come back home with me that night, then he was going to rape me all night long. He promised me that if I just let him have you, just once, then he would leave me alone and never touch me again. He said that he wouldn't hurt you. He promised. He said that he just wanted you one time. That's it. Oh, I'm sorry Savannah. I…I wasn't thinking straight. I didn't know what else to do. I was just so tired of what he was doing to me, and I'd wanted it to stop. I just wanted it to stop. You were my best friend, and I didn't want to…I was just so tired. So, so tired."

"Oh, God!" I burst into tears.

I hunched over as I cried, holding my belly.

I couldn't believe that…all of these years…what had happened to me…was all because of…Livy?

"I'm so, so sorry, Savannah. I've never been able to forgive myself," Livy continued to wail. "And when I heard you that night, screaming for me…"

"You heard me? You heard me calling out for your help?"

"Yes. I heard you. I got up. I was going to come and help you but I…I just couldn't seem to open my bedroom door. I didn't know what would happen next if I tried to help you. If I tried to stop him. I was scared. I heard you screaming, and all I could do was stand there and cry."

"Why Livy? Why would you do that to me? Me? Your best friend? I…I loved you like a sister. Why would you do that to me!"

Livy hung her head.

My heart was broken.

"I'm sorry. I've carried this horrible secret around, for so many years, and I'm just so sorry." Livy walked towards me.

Back up. Back the fuck up. Back…

Attack!

I pounced on Livy, full of rage and I started to swing.

I punched her, slapped at her and pulled her by her hair.

At first, she'd tried to defend herself, but then she just…

She just gave up.

She allowed me to hit her time and time again while she did nothing.

"You ruined my life! You ruined my life!"

I pounded on her until I was out of breath and until I saw blood. Still, she did nothing. All she did was cry.

Sweating, a face full of tears and snots coming out of my nose, finally, I pushed away from her.

With a bloody nose and busted lip, Livy cried from the deepest part of her soul. Her cries were filled with so much sorrow and pain, but I didn't care.

I would never forgive her for what she did to me!

Never!

How could I?

"I'm sorry. I'm sorry," Livy sobbed.

Breathless, I picked the car keys up from the floor, and I headed towards the front door.

"Savannah…"

"Go to Hell Livy! Just go to Hell! Go find a needle, stick it in your arm and die!" I screamed at her, and then I ran out of the house in tears, with her crying even louder than she had been before.

Blurred vision and all, I hopped into the car and pressed on the gas.

Never in a million years would I have thought that Livy intentionally brought me home with her that night to be raped.

Who does that to someone?

Especially to someone that they love?

Why would she want to put me through the same pain that she was already going through? Why would she want to ruin me too?

For the life of me, I couldn't begin to understand. And even though she'd told me why, to me, it just didn't make sense. It just wasn't right. It just wasn't fair.

I sped down the road, but I knew that I wasn't going to make it back to Grandma's. I had to stop. I just had to stop.

I swerved into the barbershop's parking lot.

All of the men turned their attention towards the car. I opened the door, and Jace smiled once he noticed that it was me, but I didn't smile back.

I ran to him.

I jumped into his arms, and I just started to cry.

"What is it? What's wrong V? Tell me what's wrong."

"Everything," I blurted out in between sobs. "Everything."

And there was nothing that anyone could do to make it right.

~***~

"I-85 is still closed."

"I know grandma."

After crying in Jace's arms the other day, I left him standing there without answering any of his questions. I'd come back to grandma's and started putting my bags in my car. And then I told her that I was leaving.

I didn't care about my cracked windshield, or the possible traffic and road issues because of the hurricane damage. I just wanted to drive as far away as I could from this evil town and the people in it. I figured once I was far enough away, I could stop somewhere to get my window fixed.

I just wanted to go.

Grandma and everyone else chased me out of the house that day. They wanted to know what was wrong. They wanted to know what happened, and why I was crying. I didn't answer them. I remember glancing at grandma, and the look on her face made me feel even worse. It was as though she knew that if I left upset, then she would never see me again. And it appeared to be breaking her heart.

Still, I drove away.

I'd hurried towards the highway, but only to be disappointed. The highway home was closed. I couldn't even get to the airport if I wanted to. Not only did they explain that trees had fallen down in various places, but also parts of the highway, some of the roads were cracked. And they explained to drivers that there were extensive damages to a few bridges too. The damage was in the opposite direction on the highway, from where Jayceon lived, which was why we hadn't known that the highway northbound was in such bad shape.

So, I didn't have a choice but to turn around and come back.

That was two days ago.

And though they were working on the highway, it was still unavailable, and I still couldn't go home. I'd tried to find an alternate route, and there were some, but all of them involved at least some kind of travel on that particular highway.

It was the only way out.

It was the only way out of hell.

I was stuck here. And I wasn't happy about it.

The only good thing that had come out of the inconvenience was that I was so full of rage that I locked myself in my old bedroom, and I took out all my frustrations on my keyboard.

I've typed so much in the last two days that I was sure that I would be finished with my book in no time.

I'm hurt. I'm angry.

And I'm a lot of other things too.

"Jayceon is worried about you."

"I know. I'll text him today."

"You wanna' tell me what happened?"

"No."

"Was it somethin' about Livy?"

I didn't say anything.

I didn't want to hear her name. I didn't want to think about her. I wish I could forget her.

After waiting a while for my response, Grandma stood up and started to tidy up the living room. After being there for a week, everyone was finally gone, but they'd left behind a big mess.

"Can you go get me the covers off the beds in those back rooms? Bring me the covers, the sheets, and the bed skirts. I'm gonna' change them all."

I stood up to go do as I was told.

I walked into what used to be Gamma's old room.

I hadn't been in there since I'd helped grandma pack up some of her things.

I pulled the covers and the sheets off the bed, and then I lifted the mattress slightly and tugged at the bed skirt. To my surprise, a journal came out with it.

Picking it up, I opened it up and saw that it was Gamma's.

The journal was kind of thick, and as I flipped through the pages, I could see by the dates that she would only write in it every once in a while. The earliest entry was from about twelve years ago. So, she'd had this same journal for a mighty long time.

I contemplated or whether or not I should take it and read it.

Journals are private. I have plenty of them, but I wrote in mine a lot more than Gamma had. And if her journal was anything like mine, there was no telling what personal things were inside of it. Maybe it would be interesting to see Gamma in a different light; even though she was gone. To get an idea of who she really was behind her hard-outer shell.

To see her as...*human.*

I grabbed the items and took the journal to the room that I slept in and placed it inside of the *one* bag that I'd brought back into the house. I wasn't taking out the rest of them because as soon as I could leave, that's exactly what I was going to do.

Just as I was about to leave the room my phone started to buzz.

Nathaniel.

"Hey, I flew to Charlotte again, but I'm stuck at the airport. I can't get to you because the highway is down."

"What? Nathaniel, why do you keep flying all this way?"

"Because this is where you are. And I was coming to make sure that you're okay."

Aww! How sweet.

I exhaled.

"I'm okay. And yes, I know about the highway. I'd tried to leave the other day, but the highway to get home is closed. They don't know when it'll be up and running again. Two bridges were badly damaged; as well as some of the road. I couldn't even make it to the airport."

"You were coming home?"

"Yes. I was coming home."

Nathaniel was quiet.

"Okay. I'll get back on a plane and fly back to New York since I can't get to you anyway. I just wanted to make sure you were okay. You weren't responding to my text messages or answering your phone, so..."

I'd been ignoring Nathaniel too, just like everyone else, for two days.

"I'm sorry. A lot has been going on, but I'm okay. And trust me, as soon as I can, I'll be coming home."

"Okay, I'll be waiting on you, Savannah. I'll be waiting on you to come home to me," Nathaniel said.

We spoke for a few more seconds, and then we said our goodbyes. Before I could entirely hang up with Nathaniel, Jace started to beep in.

"Hey, okay, now shit, I gave you some space. Don't make me come over there."

I chuckled.

"I've been calling you."

"I know. I'm sorry."

"Are you okay?"

"No. But I'm better. "

I took the handful of covers and sheets to grandma, and then I headed to sit on the back porch.

"What was going on with you? Why were you crying?"

"I rather not talk about it. How's the barbershop?"

"Not so good. It wasn't covered by insurance."

"What?"

"Harvey canceled his insurance on the building the day before I purchased it. In his defense, I did tell him that I would be calling to pick up insurance that Monday, but the insurance company hadn't allowed me to. They'd said that since the State of Emergency had been declared, I had to wait until after the hurricane."

"Can they do that?"

"I think so. I'm not sure. I just didn't expect it to get messed up like this. The roof is destroyed. The rain destroyed pretty much everything inside."

"I'm so sorry Jace."

"I won't even tell you how much it's goin' cost to get everything fixed."

"Do you need a loan?"

Why did I say that?

"Don't play me like that. I have my own money. I don't want your money. I'll figure it out. Or maybe this is a sign. Maybe this was the wrong move. Life might be trying to tell me something."

"Something like what?"

Jace chuckled. "You never know."

We talked for about five more minutes, and then I asked him to pick me up on his way home.

"I'll see you later," I said to him just as Marlo came out the back door.

"Hey."

"Hey."

She sat down beside me on the porch.

It was nearing the end of October, and it was cool. I shivered wishing that I'd slipped on my jacket.

"I heard that you'd tried to leave the other day and that you were a mess."

Marlo hadn't been there when I'd tried to leave. She'd come back later that night, and by then I was refusing to speak to anyone.

"Do you wanna' talk about it?"

"Nope."

"You wanna' talk about what you saw? You know with me and---?"

"Nope."

Marlo frowned, but I could tell she was about to explain herself anyway. "I rather sleep with him, than anyone else."

"What?"

She didn't repeat herself, but I'd heard what she'd said.

"So, let me get this straight. You don't see a problem with screwing your cousin's husband?"

Everyone in this damn town is crazy!

"I didn't say it wasn't a problem. If it's not him, then it'll be some random man every now and then. At least I know him. At least with Corbin, we have an understanding."

"What understanding? Keep fucking and don't get caught?"

Marlo looked at me. "No. Neither of us seem to get what we need at home. So, we get it from each other. We had a moment, a long time ago, where we confided in each other. We were both sexually frustrated with our spouses. So, we came up with a solution. We don't screw around all the time. Maybe once or twice a month, if that. And we don't screw other people. Just each other. And our spouses. We both still want our marriages. And though you might not understand this, or believe it, sleeping with each other has made our marriages better."

"How?"

"We're not angry all the time anymore when they can't satisfy us or give us the extra attention that we need. We just get it from each other. So, there's less tension. Less arguing and fighting. My marriage is just fine. And Corbin and Cassy are happy too."

"This is wrong, Marlo. This is wrong on so many levels. Cassy is your cousin."

"Yeah. I know."

"Do you love Corbin?"

"Of course not. I love my husband. My kids. My family."

"Why not just tell Luis what you need from him?"

"I did. He'll try to give me what I want for a while. He'll be more sexual and romantic. More spontaneous and open-minded. But it never lasts long. He always goes back to himself after a few weeks. He's a damn good man, but he leaves something to be desired in the bedroom. More times than not."

"Didn't you know that before you married him?"

"Yes. But that one thing wasn't enough to pass up on all of the other good things about him."

"So, you just rather cheat on him?"

"I don't expect you to understand. I've always loved sex, Savannah. I mean, you know that. I learned a long time ago that it's hard to find just one man to give you everything that you need. I thought pleasing myself would make up for the times that I wanted more, but it didn't. Luis and I are just on different levels sexually. We like different things. After ten years of marriage, we're still just different in that area."

"Hell, you could've fooled me. It seems like y'all are having more than enough sex. You have five kids to show for it."

Marlo looked at me, ashamed. "Two of them are Corbin's."

"What!"

I shouted so loud that it made my head hurt.

"My last two kids are his."

"No! Wait. Wait. Two of your kids are by *your* cousin's husband?"

"Yes."

"Marlo, this is crazy! Oh my God! Does he know?"

"Of course."

Unbelievable!

Corbin and Cassy only had one child, but I'd heard her say that she wanted more. She was going to lose her mind if she ever found out the truth about Marlo's kids.

I'm not a big fan of Cassy and her ways, but this is wrong. What Marlo and her husband are doing to her is wrong!

"We've been doing this for about five years. My three-year-old and the baby is his. We don't talk about it though. I told him upfront, both times, that I had a feeling that they were his kids. He asked what I wanted to do about it, and I'd told him nothing. We don't want to ruin our marriages. We both know the truth, and that's all that matters."

"But what about the kids?"

I knew firsthand how it felt to be lied to about your father.

"The kids are loved. They'll be fine. Thank God that both of them came out looking like me," Marlo stood up. "This is a small town, Vana. It's not always a lot of options. Hell, I'm pretty sure if Jace would've been interested in Cassy, she would've…"

"Yeah, but Jace and I were never married. Big difference!"

"Yes. It is. But what Corbin and I do, what we share---it works for us. It keeps us happy. It keeps our marriages afloat. And I don't see us stopping any time soon. It's our little secret. Well, I guess it's all three of ours now."

"Marlo, just think about this. I can only imagine that one day, everything will come out, and a lot of people are going to get hurt. Or worse. You're lying to your husband. And to your family."

Surprisingly, she shrugged. "Sometimes lying is the only option you have. Sometimes it's the only way to make it through. Sometimes life just doesn't work without telling a few lies or keeping a few secrets. If anyone can relate to this…it's you."

Umph. I guess.

~***~

"Savannah."

I looked up to see Sheriff Kori standing in front of me.

I was back at the coffee shop working on my book.

I'd had an amazing night with Jace, and I was feeling inspired. So, I was writing yet again.

"Hi."

He stared at me.

"Uh, I don't really know how to say this, but it looks like you're my sister after all."

"What?" As expected, I became extremely nervous. "He admitted it?"

Kori shrugged. "Not at first. My mother forced him to tell me the truth. To tell me the story."

"What story?"

"He lied to your mother. My parents are originally from Canada. They, along with a few other family members, moved down to this area in the early 80's. They started a few businesses in different states and cities. My parents started Frank's Hardware Store. It's three of them now. Anyway, at some time or another, he met your mother. He lied to her. He didn't tell her that he was married. Apparently, she couldn't bring him home to meet her family, so, being that they could only fool around in secret, it was easy for him to hide the truth. And then she got pregnant with you. Your mom had no idea that he had a wife until she spotted them together one day. And that's when both women learned the truth. Your mother approached them, and he finally told her he had a wife."

My heart broke for mama.

"Your mother told dad that she didn't want anything from him and that she would raise you on her own. And apparently, that's what she did."

He lied to her.

And she'd had to deal with the consequences alone. Mama had to listen to grandma's mouth, chastisement from nasty church folks, and with being ridiculed by people my entire childhood. And it was all because he lied to her.

"My mother forgave him. And a few years later they had me. All this time I had a sister and neither of them said a word." Kori looked disturbed. "And I made a pass at you."

"Yeah, that would've been bad."

"I've always respected him. My…*our* father taught me how to be a man. He always taught me to take care of my responsibilities. But thirty plus years ago, he walked away from his."

Sheriff Kori, my half-brother, half-smiled at me, and without saying anything else, he walked out of the coffee shop.

And I headed out right behind him.

Finally, I had a piece of the truth, but I wasn't sure what to do with it. Finally, I knew who my father was. And the truth about him and mama.

Why wasn't it enough?

And there was one thing that I didn't quite understand.

If he'd lied to her, why was she always going to see him?

It wasn't like the visits to his store were about me. Mama never allowed me to meet him. And there were a few other hardware stores in town, but she'd always gone to his.

Why?

Maybe grandma knew something.

"Mama wasn't a homewrecker after all," I said to Grandma Whinny as soon as I walked into the house.

"What? Chile what are you talkin' about?"

"He lied to her. Just like he stood in my face and lied to me. She didn't know that he was married. He lied to her. I ran into Sheriff Kori, and he told me that "our" father finally admitted the truth. He lied to mama about being married. She got pregnant, found out the truth, and told him that she didn't want anything to do with him. And apparently, my father's wife knew about me too. All this time, she knew he had a daughter, and never made him step up."

I sat down across from grandma.

"Humph. You can't make a man do anything. Chile, you should know that by now." Grandma looked at me for a while, and then she continued. "And I already knew that."

"You knew what? You knew that he lied to mama?"

"Not at first. Not for years. I didn't know the whole story. I just knew that he was married, because that was all that Glorianne told me. And then one night, while she was drunk, she let it all out. She talked about him, and how he never mentioned to her that he was married. She talked about how angry she was, and how she was the one who had to carry the burden alone."

Burden?

Was I a burden?

"She loved him. Though she knew that I would've disagreed, she said that he was the only man that she ever loved. And he hurt her. He broke her heart. That's why she never wanted to get married. She used to say that love and marriage was a joke. Lord, I would curse up a storm when she said that, but that's what she believed. And it was his fault that she felt that way."

I exhaled loudly.

"Why didn't you tell me all of this when you told me who he was?"

"Why would I? Some things are better left unsaid. Telling you that he was your daddy was more than enough. That's all you really needed to know."

"What am I supposed to do now?"

"Whatever you want to do, shug. If you want to get to know yo' *pappy*, then go on and get to know him. There's still time. And if you don't want to, then don't."

She continued to fold the towels.

"He knew about me. And he never tried to know me. He'd denied being my father right to my face. He didn't want me."

"Well, if you ask me, you turned out pretty good without him," Grandma smiled.

I guess that was one way to look at it.

They say that the truth will set you free, but baby, sometimes the truth sucks!

"Before you leave here, pay him another visit. Not for his sake. But for yours." Grandma stacked the towels, and then picked up a rag, before making her next comment. "That's what she gets for sneakin' around wit' him anyway. I love you, and I ain't got nothin' against white folks, but bloodlines ain't supposed to mix," I didn't like her comments, but I knew better than to say the wrong thing, so I said nothing. "I guess since you're a little bit of both, whichever way the wind blows you, I guess you'll be okay." Grandma shook her head.

"That sure didn't stop you from having something to say about Nathaniel."

Grandma shrugged. "You didn't know the truth then. So, I had to play the part."

I turned away from her so that I could roll my eyes.

"You know what, honestly, I'd always wanted yo' mama to get with Harvey," she said.

I cringed.

"He was a nice boy, and he chased after yo' mama sort of like how Jayceon used to chase after you. She never liked him though. She let that good man slip right through her fingers and marry someone else. I always told her that she'd missed out on her blessing. She missed out on that good man."

"Harvey is NOT a good man!" I turned to look at her.

"First of all, who in the hell are you hollerin' at?" She asked me.

"Sorry."

She glared at me. "And Harvey is—"

"Harvey isn't a good man, grandma," I interrupted her. "He...raped Livy. And..."

162

I stopped. She stared at me with wide eyes. Her chest moved up and down rapidly, and her breathing had picked up as a result of me sharing Livy's secret with her. If I told her that he raped me too, it would surely give her a heart attack.

"And he ruined her. Harvey is not a good man," I mumbled instead. As she'd said: Some things are just better left unsaid.

~***~

"What if I go with you."

Jace rubbed the side of my face.

"Go where?"

I was back at Jace's house.

I had to get away from grandma. After telling her about Livy, she had tons of questions. She'd wanted to talk about it over and over again. She was pissed! She promised not to tell Livy that I'd told her, and she promised that she wouldn't tell anyone else. But she said that she couldn't guarantee that she wouldn't slap the shit out of Harvey whenever she saw him again.

"Back to New York."

I sat up in the bed.

"I mean, I can be a barber anywhere. It's thirty-grand to get everything with the barbershop either rebuilt or fixed. I'm gonna' be looking for a new building anyway. Why not look in New York?"

"Uh, what about...Yasmine?"

"The good thing about being your own boss is that you can work when you want to. I can come home all the time. Summertime, if it's okay with you, she can come to visit us. We can make this work. We can start over...in New York. I know that's where you wanna' be. I know you're not going to stay here. I just keep thinking that it all happened for a reason and now that I have you back, I don't want to lose you again."

Wow.

"Um, who said you had me back?" I smiled at him.

"Thirty-minutes ago, when I was giving you this *business*, you were saying a whole lot stuff."

"Jace!" Playfully, I slapped his arm. "I mean whatever this is, it has been amazing. I don't really know what to say."

"Just say you love me."

Beaming at him I said, "I love you."

And honestly, I felt like I did.

Everything that I'd felt for him in the past was back, times ten. Maybe we were moving too fast. Or maybe it was fate. I couldn't be sure. I could only be honest with myself. With everything that had come out since I'd been back in town, all the secrets and truths, Jace had been like my own little ray of sunshine.

"That's all I needed to hear."

The doorbell sounded, and Jace got out of the bed and slipped on a pair of shorts. He disappeared out of the room, and I checked my phone.

Nathaniel had messaged me a few times.

He was concerned about me, and he too was talking about us. He wanted to get back together. He wanted another chance.

What am I going to do?

I never thought that Jace would want to leave here. I just assumed that one day, whatever this was would come to an end. Now, he was willing to go to New York with me.

New York...where Nathaniel was waiting for me.

I texted Nathaniel, and then I got up and slipped on a t-shirt. I headed to go see what Jace was doing, but I stopped in the hallway, once I heard his ex-wife's voice.

"We're going to take her to *Trunk-Or-Treat* at a few churches."

It was Halloween.

"You're such a pretty princess," Jace complimented his daughter.

"Thank you, Daddy."

"Where's your little girlfriend?" I heard Reeva ask him.

"Stop."

"Stop what? I see why you couldn't fully love me all these years. No matter how much I look like her, I just wasn't her."

"Have a good time tonight, okay Yas? Call Daddy as soon as you get home," Jace ignored her comment, and the next sound I heard was the front door closing.

I made my way into the living room.

"Did you really compare her to me?"

"No. I told her about you. I told her how much you meant to me and that you left me, but I loved her for her. I married her because I loved her. It didn't have anything to do with you."

"Well, she doesn't seem to think so."

"Well, it's true."

"You have to admit that we do look alike…a lot!"

"Really? I hadn't notice," Jace said as he picked me up. He walked towards the bedroom with me in his arms.

"Our birthdays are next week. Want to spend them together?"

"Aw man, do I have to?"

Jace grinned as he kissed me. "And in the meantime, I'll be making plans. Plans to leave here with you," Jace kissed me again, and then his kisses led to everything else.

The night went by smoothly, and once Jace fell asleep, I found myself staring at him. And though I still felt something for Nathaniel, I couldn't be sure if it was more than what I was feeling for Jace. I was in love with him.

Maybe this was all a part of a higher plan. Maybe this was how things were supposed to be. Maybe since the very beginning, we had been meant to be.

Maybe.

"The highway is open," Grandma said once I walked through the front door the next morning.

"Good."

"So, I guess you'll be leaving now."

"Not yet. I'll be staying until after my birthday."

"Jayceon?"

"Yes."

"Um um, be careful now. You might end up staying forever."

"Trust me, I won't."

"The cops are outside!" Uncle Willie yelled.

"Boy shut up! *Ain't* no damn cops outside!" Grandma yelled back at him.

I looked out the front door.

"Actually grandma, there is."

I saw Sheriff Kori get out of his car.

Grandma followed behind me out the front door.

Once I was on the front porch, Kori looked at me. I couldn't read his facial expression, so I waited for him to speak.

"I uh, I just wanted to come by and tell you that we're reopening your mother's murder case. Some new evidence has been discovered."

My heart dropped.

The police are reopening her murder case?

After fifteen years?

"What, um, what new evidence?"

"I'm not at liberty to say at this time. We may have a few questions for you so if possible…stick around."

My brother turned away from me, just as grandma pulled me close to her and wrapped her arms around me.

For fifteen years, the same question has always been in the back of my mind.

Who killed my mother?

Dear God, please let them find her killer this time.

****

CHAPTER SIX

"Can we celebrate the day before your birthday?"

My birthday was November 5th. Jace's was the 6th.

"My daughter has a dance competition on your birthday. And it's four hours away. Reeva has a meeting and can't go. So, I'll be taking her."

"Oh, it's fine. I understand. Sure."

"Cool. You can come with us if you want."

"Oh no, I think I'll pass."

Jace laughed in my ear. "So, how are you feeling about…"

"Yeah. I don't know."

My brother had yet to tell me exactly what evidence they'd found to reopen my mother's case, but I didn't care. I've waited years for answers on what really happened to mama that night, and I was praying that I finally got them.

"It took years for me to get over her death. Even after I left here, I thought about her all the time. She wasn't the best mother. Lord knows she wasn't. But she was mine. And for someone to just do something like that to her, and leave her there…"

"Everything is gonna' be okay," Jace confirmed.

"I hope so."

Unfortunately, I was staying in Clover, even after my birthday, because I wasn't going anywhere until they either found mama's killer or closed the case again.

"Grandma Whinny!"

Cassy rushed through the front door with her baby hanging on to her for dear life. She startled me.

"Jace, I'll call you right back."

Cassy glanced at me, and then she yelled for grandma again.

"Chile! Have you lost yo' damn mind? Why are you screamin' like that? And look at how you are holdin' that baby! Give her to me!" Grandma demanded, and Cassy somewhat threw the baby into her arms.

"We need to stay here for a while. My husband…Corbin…is having an affair! He's cheating on me!"

Uh oh.

My heart started to race.

Cassy flopped down on the other end of the couch. I tried not to make eye contact with her. I didn't want her to suspect that I knew anything.

"What? Are you sure?"

"Yes, I'm sure. I found the receipts from the hotel, and I flipped out on him. Finally, he broke down and admitted to having an affair, but he won't tell me who it's with."

Cassy started to sob.

She was hurting.

She was hurting because of Marlo.

"What am I supposed to do?" She asked grandma.

"Well, the only thing you can do is choose. You can choose to stay. Or you can choose to leave. But you have to make a choice. And no one can tell you what choice to make," Grandma kissed the baby. "Or you can choose to kill him."

Cassy and I both looked at her.

"I'm just kidding."

Yeah right.

"You can choose to fight Cass," I commented.

"What? I don't think you have room to give anyone advice on marriage. Aren't you divorced?" She snarled.

"That's exactly why I *can* give you some advice, smart ass! Because I am divorced. I've been through where you're headed. And for the record, my husband left me. He didn't have an affair. He didn't cheat on me. But had I fought for my marriage, had I listened to what he was saying to me, had I heard what he needed from me, then we would still be married to this day. What you need to figure out is what he's saying to you that you're not listening to. What is he asking you for that you're not giving him? It doesn't make what he did to you right, and it doesn't mean that he won't do it again, but maybe there's something that you can do to get your marriage back on the right track. Fight for your husband and your marriage. Figure out what's missing. See if there's something that you could do. That's what I would do. That's what I should've done. Who knows, the woman he's sleeping with might be *giving* him the things that he's afraid to ask you for. Or maybe she does the things you *won't* do."

"You sure yo' husband didn't cheat on you, girl?" Grandma Whinny asked me. She looked at me, suspiciously. As though she was trying to read my mind.

"I'm sure. Just…just…sometimes it's an easy fix."

Cassy scrunched up her face. "Grandma, I like your idea better. How do I kill him?"

We all let out a chuckle, and I wiped the sweat from my forehead. I noticed that grandma was still staring at me.

I felt guilty because I knew the truth and I couldn't say anything.

After talking for a little while longer, Cassy's phone rang, and she excused herself to go argue with Corbin.

"What do you know?" Grandma grilled me as soon as Cassy was out of sight.

"Huh?"

"If you can huh, you can hear! You know something, don't you?"

"Me? No. What would I know? Cassy and I barely get along, and I haven't said more than three sentences to her husband. I don't know anything. I was just trying to help her out. Divorce is hard."

"It's supposed to be. Now, which one is it?"

"Which one is what?"

"Which one of your triflin' ass cousins is screwing your other cousin's husband?"

What? How did she know?

"What?"

Grandma glared at me. "I can tell that you know somethin'. You don't want to be in the middle. But fine. Don't tell me. You just tell her...whichever *heffa'* it is, that if it ever comes out, I'm gonna' beat her ass! Now, come on baby, let's go get you somethin' to eat."

Grandma kissed the baby and headed for the kitchen.

With Cassy screaming at the top of her lungs, I got up to go outside to call Marlo.

"Oh!" I grabbed my chest.

"Sorry. I didn't mean to startle you."

A man in a suit had been standing right in front of the door when I opened it.

I stepped outside.

"Ms. Savannah Lynch?"

"Yes."

"I'm Detective Brent Moss. I wanted to ask you a few things if you don't mind, about your mother's murder."

"Sheriff Kori is working this case, right?"

"Right. And so am I. He needed some help. So, here I am. I know that you spoke with officers back then. You're older now. So, I wanted to talk to you again. Maybe you can remember something now that you couldn't during that time. Maybe you can put together some things that you were too young to put together then."

I sat down on the front porch. The detective stood directly in front of me.

"Can you tell me what they found? The new evidence?"

"I can't give out that information at this time. How did your mother seem that last time that you saw her alive?"

I remember being asked this question fifteen years ago, but I was willing to answer it again. I would answer anything that they asked me.

"She seemed normal. She helped me prepare for homecoming, and then she went to work. That was the last time that I saw her."

"And she didn't seem worried or bothered by anything?"

"No."

"What about the days leading up to her death? Was she acting like herself? Did you see her arguing with anyone?"

"No. Mama didn't have many friends. She only dealt with family. And she never really had a stable man in her life. She never had "boyfriend" drama. Not any that she let me see anyway."

"What about your father?"

I exhaled loudly. "Well, I just found out who he is. I grew up without him. I never met him, until recently. And even then, he didn't claim me. Frank. He owns that big hardware store on Armstrong Drive. He's married. He was married then too. When mama got pregnant with me."

"Frank's Hardware Store? Isn't that…"

"Yes. Sheriff Kori's father. Apparently, he's my half-brother."

"Wow."

"Yeah. Tell me about it."

"And you just recently found this out? And you never saw the two of them together? Frank and your mother?"

"Yes. I just found out. And I never saw them together. But we always went by his store. From what has been told to me, after my mother found out that he was married, she told him that she didn't want anything to do with him. She never let him see me. Yet, I remember going by his store all the time. I never went inside. She always told me to stay in the car, but she always went in."

"Interesting." The detective wrote something down in the notepad that he'd pulled out of his pocket. "And what about his wife? Does she know that you are his daughter?"

"She knew the whole time. She found out about the affair the same day that mama found out that he was married. She decided to stay with him."

"Maybe he was giving your mother money to help take care of you. Maybe they were still fooling around. Maybe that's why she always went to the store."

I shrugged. "Maybe."

"I wonder if Frank's wife knew about the frequent store visits. I wonder if she thought they were still having an affair."

Hmm…

"It wasn't an affair. He lied to her."

"Initially. But if she continued to sleep with him, after discovering that he was married, then it was indeed an affair."

"I guess it would be. *If* that's the case."

"Frank, nor his wife, were questioned back then. I'll be sure to speak to them this time around. Seems worth looking into."

So many thoughts were floating around inside my head.

What if mama had still been messing around with my daddy?

What if his wife found out?

What if…

"Anything else that you can think of? That you know now that you didn't know then?"

I thought for a second.

"Harvey."

"Harvey? I've heard his name. Harvey? The barber?"

"Yes. Was he questioned last time?"

The detective looked in his notepad. "No. I'm afraid he wasn't. Should he be questioned?"

"Since I've been back, I've heard that he had a thing for my mother. I heard that he was obsessed with her and that once he came on to her and she threw her drink in his face at a bar. He's my best…an old friend's step-father and he isn't the nice man that everyone thinks he is."

"Noted. I'll check into him as well."

I nodded.

I wanted to tell him the comment that Harvey said to me all of those years ago. The one where he threatened to kill me if I told anyone about what he'd done to me. But I couldn't tell one part, without telling it all. So, I said nothing.

"I'll let you know if I have any more questions for you and if you think of anything else, please give me a call."

He handed me his card.

The detective hopped off the porch, since the steps were still messed up, and I watched his car until it disappeared.

"They're goin' to find her killer this time. I can feel it in my bones."

Grandma was standing in the door.

"Yeah," I responded to her.

I could feel it too.

~***~

"Why you gotta' be so damn fine?"

I blushed.

Jace opened his truck's door, and I got inside.

Once he was seated, I smiled at him. "Okay, where are we going?"

"You're overdressed."

"What?"

I looked down at my outfit. Jace told me to be ready by seven. I guess I assumed that we would be going to dinner.

"Where are we going?"

"You remember the second night that we were stuck inside together, after the hurricane?"

"Yes."

"What's one of the things you told me that you've always wanted to do? You were my biggest fan in high school, and to this day…"

"Football!"

Jace smiled.

"You're taking me to a football game?"

"Yep. It's Sunday night football in Charlotte tonight. I got us some good seats too. Close to the field."

"Oh my God!"

I love football.

I used to love watching Jace play, and I've been a *Panthers* fan for as long as I could remember, but I've never been to one of their football games.

"If you want to do dinner and something more romantic, I made reservations for that too. Just in case."

"No! I want to go to the game. It's perfect. It's thoughtful and sweet."

Jace kept one hand on the wheel as he reached into the backseat. He handed me a bag.

I looked inside it to see that it was a *Panthers* jersey, a pair of jeans and he told me that he'd gotten me a new pair of sneakers that were still in the backseat.

"I knew you were going to overdress."

This man!

He was always one step ahead.

I love him.

I undressed as he drove and after teasing him a little, I slipped on the jeans and the jersey.

We arrived at the stadium, and after the longest walk of my life, finally, we made it to our seats just as they started to sing the *National Anthem*.

I was on cloud nine.

The lights.

The noise.

I'd never been so nervous, excited and overwhelmed all at the same time.

Jace grabbed my hand.

"Happy Early Birthday V. I love you," he said.

I mouthed the words back to him, and then I turned my attention towards the field.

I was ready for some football!

The entire game I was fired up.

I screamed. I cheered. I had the time of my life!

Jace just smiled at me the whole time. I caught him staring at me, often, and when I would ask him what he was looking at, he would say nothing.

I truly enjoyed myself, and not to mention *we* won!

Once the game was over, it took a while to make it through the crowd, but now, we were back in the parking lot and making our way towards Jace's truck.

"This is one of the best birthdays, well birthday gifts that I've had in a very long time."

"Really? Well, I'm trying to make it the best birthday EVER." Jace stopped walking and touched my arm.

Right there, in the parking lot, all six-feet of him got down on one knee.

"Jace get up. What are you doing—what---"

I touched my chest just as Jace removed the black velvet box from his pocket.

"Jace, what are you doing? What are you doing?"

"I've loved you for as long as I can remember. It was always you. You were the girl of my dreams back then. And the woman of my dreams now. It has always been you. I don't want to live without you. I can't lose you again. I won't lose you again. I know this might be strange or too soon, but we can spend forever falling in love again. If you just say yes."

I was speechless.

Never in a million years could I have imagined that I would be here, at this moment, with Jace of all people, but here I was.

Here I was with my first love down on one knee wanting to spend the rest of his life with me. Asking to marry me.

"Don't worry about anything. I'm ready to sell my house. I've been looking at barbershops in New York. If that's where you want to be that's where I'll be too. Just say yes V. All you gotta' do is say yes. Savannah Lynch, will you marry me?"

There was a crowd of people looking on. Cars had stopped, and the drivers had gotten out to watch.

I felt as though I couldn't breathe.

My heart was so full.

My heart was so happy.

I took a deep breath, just as I started to nod.

"Yes…"

"Yes?" Jace repeated.

"Yes."

The crowd roared as he placed the ring on my finger, and as soon as Jace was on his feet, he kissed me, picked me up and started to spin me around in his arms.

I threw my head back in laughter, and once he put me down, I looked at the ring in awe. "I love you," I blubbered.

"Always?"

Smiling at him, I nodded. "Forever."

Oh my God!

I'm getting married!

Again.

And to Jace!

~***~

"What is that on your finger?" Cassy roared.

I'd just walked in the door from being with Jace all night, and I was still on cloud nine.

I couldn't believe that he'd proposed.

And I couldn't believe that I'd said yes.

We'd spent all night making love and making plans.

I'd meant to take off the ring. I wasn't prepared to tell anyone just yet, but I forgot.

"Uh, Jace gave me a promise ring."

"A promise ring? Y'all too damn old for promise rings," Cassy took a closer look at it. "But damn! That's one hell of a promise. Grandma, look at this ring."

Grandma Whinny leaned over to take a look.

"It sho' is. Looks like an engagement ring to me," She probed. "So, does this mean you're staying?"

"No. It's just a promise ring. And if we decide to get serious, he's going to move to New York."

"Really?"

"Yes."

"I wonder what the Pastor is going to have to say about that."

I took the ring off and put it in my pocket to avoid any more questions, and to change the subject.

A knock on the door caused me to turn around, but Cassy jumped up and headed for it.

Grandma and I started to chat, and once she smiled, I turned around to see what she was grinning at.

Nathaniel.

He was holding at least fifty long-stemmed roses, and just as many balloons.

"Happy birthday, baby."

"Nathaniel?"

I approached him, and he reached me what he could, and I hugged him through the rest.

"What are you doing here?"

"It's your birthday. I know you told me that you were going to stick around here because they reopened your mother's murder case, so I decided to come to you."

Cassy had a funny expression on her face.

She better not say a damn thing about Jace!

"Nice to see you again," Nathaniel spoke to grandma.

She nodded and smiled at him.

"Can we talk outside for a minute?"

Nathaniel and I placed all of the roses on the sofa, and he let go of the balloons.

"I'm surprised to see you."

That was nothing but the truth.

"I brought something for you."

Nathaniel pulled out a box.

Oh no. Oh no. Oh no!

He opened it.

It was my old wedding ring.

The ring had been in his family for years. During the divorce proceedings, he had requested it back since it had been passed down to wives in his family for over a hundred years.

"We haven't had a lot of time to talk about us. Or about what I said to you last time I was here. But I love you Savannah, and I miss you. I want you to know that I brought this because one day, I want to be able to place this ring back on your finger. I want us to give *us* another try. We were perfect together. We were complete. And I'll do anything I have to do to get us back to where we used to be."

A year ago, this was all I wanted to hear.

I never wanted to get a divorce.

And now...

Everything has changed.

"Nathaniel."

"I'm not asking you to say yes right now. Right now, I'm asking you to have dinner with me. Tonight. My new assistant has been to Charlotte a few times and suggested a few places to me. I think I picked the perfect restaurant. One I know you'll love, and I want to take you out for your birthday."

His blue eyes were like kryptonite.

It was as though I couldn't say no to him.

"Okay."

"Okay. I'm staying at the same hotel. I'll come back and get you around 8."

Nathaniel hopped off the porch and opened the door of his rental car. Of course, he knew my style and my sizes. We'd been married for years, so I wasn't surprised when he pulled out a red dress from my favorite Manhattan boutique and matching shoes.

"I have a few more gifts. This is just to start."

Nathaniel kissed me on my cheek, and I just stood there, wondering how in the world I was going to break his heart.

I had to tell him.

I had to tell him that I was in love with Jace.

I had to tell him that I was getting married to someone else.

"Umph, you must have a magic pussy. You have your first love and your ex-husband falling all over you. It must be nice," Cassy said behind me.

No! It wasn't.

It was confusing as hell!

I walked past her and watched the clock for the next few hours, trying to figure out the right words to say to Nathaniel at dinner.

Jace checked in to tell me that his daughter's team won the competition and that they would be getting back on the road to come home in the morning. I encouraged him to get in some quality time with his daughter so that he wouldn't call while I was out with Nathaniel.

Finally, after waiting around all day, it was time to get dressed.

"Sexy," Cassy said.

"Thank you."

Just as the words escaped her lips, Marlo walked into the house.

"Ooh, don't you look snazzy. Going out with Jace?"

"Nope. Her ex-husband," Cassy chimed in.

The two of them, in the same room, made me nervous.

"Oh, he's back in town? Looks like he wants you back. Have you told him about you and Jace?"

"Nope," Cassy answered for me again.

"Uh oh. Well, I just came by to tell you happy birthday."

"Thank you. I called and texted you the other day."

"I know. I've been busy with Luis and the kids," Marlo walked towards the door. I followed her outside onto the porch.

"She knows he's having an affair," I whispered.

"What?"

"She doesn't know it's you, but she knows it's someone. Corbin admitted it. She left him. Didn't he tell you?"

"No. It's not like we talk all day or even every day. We only talk when..."

I saw the lights at the top of the gravel driveway.

"Well, you ruined your cousin's marriage. Good job."

Marlo didn't respond.

She helped me step off the porch in my heels, just as Nathaniel got out of the rental.

"Hello," he said to her.

"Hi."

He turned towards me. "Hello, beautiful."

I smiled at him as he took my hand.

"Goodnight Marlo," I said to her, and then I looked into Nathaniel's eyes.

"Tonight is your night, baby," he said.

I found it hard to speak out of fear of saying the wrong thing or saying the right thing too soon.

Nathaniel opened the car door, and I picked up the gift from the seat. After getting comfortable, I opened the box.

"Aww."

It was a photo album.

On the front of the album was a picture.

A picture that I didn't know that he had. It was from the day that I'd become Editor and Chief.

I remember calling him that day. I was so excited about the promotion. He'd gotten off work and come to the office to join the celebration. Apparently, he'd taken this picture of me before I'd noticed him. I had the biggest smile on my face.

Flipping through the album, there were so many off guard photos that he had of me. Some of them while I was sleeping. Some while I was working in my office back home. Some of me with friends. None of which I'd known he'd taken, but in every one of them I looked so happy.

And then at the end, there were some photos of us. Some from the very beginning of our relationship that even I didn't have. The very last photograph in the album was of me on our wedding day. I knew it was that day because the small white flower buds were still in my hair. I was asleep on his chest, clearly exhausted after the long day, but he was awake. His lips were against my forehead, and I seemed to be sleeping with a smile on my face. He'd captured one of the sweetest, most intimate moments of us. And he'd never shared this beautiful moment with me.

Until now.

"These are beautiful."

"I used to love taking pictures of you when you weren't paying attention. It always made me appreciate your beauty just a little bit more. I can't believe I let you go. You're the best part, Savannah. The best part of life. The best part of me."

Ugh!

Why the hell am I crying?

Tears fell from my eyes. I would be lying to myself if I said that I didn't still have deep feelings for him. He's all I've had and known for so long.

"I never got to say I'm sorry," I said to him. Nathaniel started to drive. "I'm sorry that I didn't care about what you wanted and needed from me. I'm sorry that I didn't do my part or keep my promises to you."

"I'm sorry for trying to force you to. I guess I thought a child would complete us. I just wanted something that was a piece of both of us."

"I know."

"But I was wrong for walking out on you. No matter what. That wasn't the way to handle it. I see that now."

Nathaniel reached for my hand.

I exhaled, and then placed my hand inside his.

We listened to music, hand in hand, as he followed the GPS for a while and then finally, we arrived at a French restaurant in downtown Charlotte.

It was a chilly night, and though it was a weekday, there were plenty of people out walking the streets.

"Smith," Nathaniel said once we were inside.

That used to be my last name.

I was going to keep it, after the divorce, but I'd decided to go back to Lynch.

The waiter led us to our table.

"Aww."

I wasn't sure how he'd accomplished it, but there were more roses on the table than there was supposed to be. Also, I saw candles, wine, and chocolate covered strawberries as well.

It was the only table like that in the entire restaurant.

Once we were seated, the waiter told us that the wine was chilled and asked if I wanted him to pour me a glass.

"This is so nice. And you know I love French food."

"Yes. I know."

The waiter poured the wine and then told us that he would give us a minute to look over the menu.

I caught a glimpse of the look on Nathaniel's face as he looked at me.

How in the world am I going to tell him?

"So, Nathaniel, there's so much that's been going on since I got here. And..."

"Wait. Let me show you something."

Nathaniel pulled out his cell phone.

He scrolled for a second, and then he reached his phone to me. I looked at it.

"Wait...is that...I know you didn't! I know you didn't!"

"Oh yes, I did."

I'd asked him for a white baby grand piano a few months before we'd started to argue about having a baby. I'd always wanted to learn how to play the piano. I kept telling myself that if I had one at home then I would get serious about getting lessons.

"How..."

"You still keep the spare key in the same place. I went by and had it delivered."

The piano was in the center of my Zen Room. He'd placed red roses all over it, and I could see petals on the floor.

"Happy Birthday Savannah."

"This is so...I don't know what to say. Thank you, Nathaniel. Thank you so much."

"You're welcome. Now, can we just enjoy each other for a while? Eat good and catch up?"

I nodded. "Yes. We can do that."

Nathaniel kicked off the conversation. He filled me in on what had been happening with him at work. He filled me in on his family and on our mutual friends. I hadn't really spoken to any of them. Not as much as I usually would. I would send them text messages, here and there, just to let them know that I was okay.

Nathaniel told jokes and made me laugh.

He showered me with compliments, and he asked about my book. He seemed so interested in it and even gave me a few pointers. He always believed in me. He'd always encouraged me to go after my dreams. He had always been my biggest cheerleader. My family. My friend.

How was I going to give him up?

Did I really want to?

Was I really sure?

About Jace?

About the proposal?

"Happy birthday to you. Happy birthday to you!"

A group full of waiters gathered around the table with a slice of chocolate cake. It had a sparkling candle sticking out of it. They finished singing and then they all clapped after sitting the cake in front of me.

"Make a wish."

I closed my eyes.

What did I want?

What should I wish for?

Once I opened my eyes, they removed the candle and then they left Nathaniel and me to enjoy the cake.

"I want to kiss you."

"Then kiss me."

Why did I just say that?

Nathaniel smiled and started to lean in but...

"Savannah…right?"

I looked up.

It was Reeva. Jace's ex-wife.

Oh shit!

"Uh yes. How are you?"

She looked at Nathaniel. "I'm doing just fine."

"Nathaniel, this is Jace's ex-wife, Reeva. Reeva this is my ex-husband Nathaniel."

"Nice to meet you." They both said in unison.

"I spoke to Jace earlier. Tell Yasmine that I said congratulations."

"You can tell her yourself. You and Jace are dating…right?"

Bitch.

"Hmm, right. Well, you have a good night."

"Likewise," she smirked and then she walked away.

I took a deep breath before looking at Nathaniel.

"Dating?"

"He and I have been hanging out a little, well a lot, since I've been here."

"That's why he was at your grandmother's house that day?"

"Yes."

"Is it serious? I get a vibe from her like it is."

"I'm not sure what it is. We do have a lot of history."

"We have history too, Savannah."

"Yes. We do."

This was the perfect moment to tell him the truth, but I couldn't. I could tell by the look in his eyes that he was either hurt, annoyed or both.

The rest of dinner was awkward.

Finally, we stood to leave.

We walked out of the restaurant to find a horse and carriage waiting for us.

"I set this up before…we don't have to do it."

"Yes. I would love to ride it with you."

Nathaniel had put so much thought into the night that I was speechless as to how much he was able to get done. He'd done everything he could think of to make my birthday special.

"You can hold my hand."

"I don't want to step on anyone's toes."

"Nathaniel, it's not like that. And we're divorced. When I came here as far as I knew you were still expecting a baby with someone else. You and I are friends. Jace and I are friends," I lied.

I could tell that he wasn't buying it, but I concluded that tonight wasn't the right time to tell him the truth.

I could feel my phone vibrating over and over again in my small purse.

It was probably Jace.

I was sure that Reeva had called him and told him that she'd seen me on a date with my ex-husband.

I ignored my phone and forced Nathaniel to communicate with me on the ride. Once we were back at the car, I could tell that Nathaniel was forcing himself to act as though nothing was wrong. He was trying not to ask me anything else about Jace.

For the most part, he drove me back to the plantation house in silence. When we arrived, he got out of the car and walked me to the front door.

"I really had a wonderful night. Thank you for everything."

"You're welcome."

"How long are you staying?"

"I'd planned to stay a few days. Just to be here with you, but I think I'll head back to the airport tonight."

"Nathaniel."

"No. It's fine Savannah. Really. I'm fine. Enjoy the rest of your night. I love you," he said from the heart.

And then Nathaniel turned his back to me.

For some reason, it felt as though he was walking out on me and divorcing me all over again.

I was more confused than I've ever been in my entire life. It became clear to me that there were a lot of feelings for Nathaniel still there. And that no matter how much I was falling for Jace, maybe I wasn't ready to get married.

Maybe it was too fast and too soon.

Or maybe I just had to get over the fact that I had to let Nathaniel go. And maybe I didn't want to.

My phone started to vibrate again just as Nathaniel's rental disappeared. I pulled my phone out of my purse, and it was who I expected it to be.

Jace.

~***~

"That's your daddy's wife," Jace said to me.

We were at the coffee shop. I'd gone there to write again, and Jace had stopped by to see me.

The older, well-dress lady saw Jace point at her. She looked at him, and then she looked at me. I could tell that she knew exactly who I was.

After getting her coffee, she hurried out of the shop. Through the window, I watched her get into her Range Rover in a hurry, and then she sped away.

I turned my attention back to Jace.

The other night, he'd asked me about Nathaniel. I explained to him that Nathaniel popped up to surprise me for my birthday. I told him that Nathaniel took me out to dinner, and that nothing happened. Jace asked me if I told Nathaniel about the engagement. I was honest and told him no. I told him that I hadn't told anyone and that I wasn't ready to tell them just yet.

Surprisingly, he wasn't as upset as I thought he would be. He just asked questions, and once I answered them, whether it was with the truth or a lie, he let it go.

As for what I was feeling, I still wasn't sure. I was praying for a sign. Hopefully, I would get one soon.

"Looks to me like she knows who you are," Jace said.

"Apparently."

I'd never met her before. And I couldn't remember ever seeing her, even when I was younger.

Jace glanced down at his phone. "Harvey is meeting me here."

"For what!"

Jace looked at me as though I'd lost my mind.

"Damn. He's coming to bring me a few papers. What do you have against Harvey?"

"What do you mean? Nothing." I lied.

Jace searched my face for answers, but I didn't show him anything.

"So, I stopped by the church before I came here. The police are there talking to my folks."

"About mama?"

"Yeah. I think so."

"Why?"

"I don't know. They were finishing up when I came in."

I wondered where this detective was the first time around. Grandma told me that he'd come by the house again. This time, he'd come to talk to her. Detective Brent was determined to find answers. And I was hoping that he did.

"Someone is going to buy the barbershop, well, what's left of it. I guess you can say they just want the land. They're gonna' knock the barbershop down and build a laundromat."

I stared at Jace and waited for him to continue.

"One thing down. One thing to go."

He was serious about moving to New York. He was serious about giving up everything to be with me. He was determined to marry me and spend the rest of his life with me.

And so was Nathaniel.

Nathaniel called me once he was back in Manhattan, and basically, he asked me to choose him, more or less. He explained to me why he felt like we deserved another chance. He told me how much he loved me and that he couldn't live without me.

I told him that I needed some time to think.

But I couldn't do that with Jace in my face and in my space. And I liked him there. I loved having him around.

"Your brother."

I turned around to see Kori coming into the shop.

He didn't notice us until after he'd gotten his coffee.

"Savannah."

"Kori."

He nodded at Jace.

"Any luck yet with my mother's case?"

"Not yet. My parents were questioned. As a result of some comments you made."

I couldn't tell if he was bothered by what I'd told the detective or not.

Kori opened his mouth to say something, but suddenly he dropped his coffee and ran towards the door. I looked towards the window.

What?

It was Livy.

And she was holding a gun and pointing it at Harvey.

I rushed out the door with Jace behind me.

"Put the gun down!" Kori yelled. He had his gun drawn and pointing at her.

Livy was shaking.

"Drop the gun, Livy!"

She kept her eyes on Harvey.

He was smirking at her, with his hands in the air.

"Livy!" I screamed at her. "Livy. What are you doing? Put the gun down."

"Savannah?" She asked, but she didn't take her eyes off Harvey and Kori.

I held my hand up at Kori.

"Please. Don't shoot her. Livy. Put the gun down," I begged.

"No Savannah. He deserves to die. You know that he deserves to die!"

"I know he does Livy. I know. But he isn't worth it. Come on, give me the gun."

Livy didn't reply.

All of the anger that I felt towards her, at that moment, was gone.

"You don't want to go to jail, do you? Not over him, Livy."

"I don't care about jail! I don't have anything to live for anyway."

"You have me."

"You hate me."

"I don't hate you, Livy. I don't hate you. Just put the gun down."

"He ruined my life. I'm tired of being sad. I'm tired of hurting. He should be the one suffering! Not me!"

"I understand Livy. You know I understand. Please. Just give me the gun."

Jace called out my name, but I didn't answer him.

There were people in every direction, but I kept my focus on her.

I was scared.

I just wanted to save her. I just wanted her to be safe.

"Livy, you look crazy out here in front of all these people." Harvey barked.

Damn it!

Why did he have to open his mouth?

"I don't look crazy! And if I am, it's because you made me that way! Tell them what you did! Tell everyone that you're a rapist!"

Suddenly, the crowd roared with chatter.

"She's lying," Harvey said calmly.

"I'm lying! Tell them what you did to me! Tell them what you did to Savannah! Tell them that you raped us!"

No!

I wanted to scream.

She said it.

She said it in front of everyone.

She told the entire world my secret.

She told the truth about what happened to me.

It seemed as though all eyes turned to me. Even Kori's eyes glanced in my direction. I couldn't see Jace because he was behind me, but I was sure that he was looking at me too.

I felt naked. Ashamed. I wanted to run and hide, but I couldn't. Not without Livy.

"Tell the truth, Harvey! Tell the truth!"

He didn't say anything.

"Livy! Put the gun down!" Kori screamed again.

"Please Livy. Please."

I was almost to her. I'd been taking small steps in her direction, and I was almost there.

"I have to do this Savannah. I have to do this for me. For you. I need peace. I just need a little peace."

"Livy please."

"Savannah."

"Yes."

"I'm...I'm...I'm sorry," she said, and before I could say anything else she squeezed the trigger and then...

"No!"

I yelled at Kori at the sound of the bang. Livy went down to the ground. Kori looked behind him. It hadn't been him who had shot her. It was another officer who none of us had noticed on the scene.

He'd pulled the trigger.

He'd shot my *best friend*.

Harvey hunched over.

The bullet from Livy's gun hit him in either the arm or the shoulder, but unfortunately, he was going to live. People surrounded him, just as I fell to my knees to hold Livy.

The officer's bullet had hit her in the chest.

Blood was coming out of her mouth, and she was struggling to look at me. "No! No! No! Livy."

I rocked her.

"Sa...Sa..." She tried to mutter, but she couldn't get out the words. Instead, she grabbed my hand. I started to cry.

"I forgive you, Livy. I forgive you," I cried.

Livy found a way to smile at me and then...she died.

****

CHAPTER SEVEN

"Why didn't you tell me!" Grandma yelled at me.

I was a mess.

I just sat there.

Jace sat close to me.

All night he'd stayed right there, and he wouldn't leave my side.

"Vana, why wouldn't you tell me!"

"I don't know," I said softly.

I was sad.

"Why didn't you…"

"I said I don't fucking know!" I yelled.

The whole room got quiet, even grandma.

"Do you think I wanted everyone to know that Harvey raped me? Do you? I didn't say anything because I was ashamed! Okay! I was embarrassed! I felt dirty and violated, and I didn't want anyone to know!"

I started to sob.

Jace pulled me close to him.

I didn't bother looking around the room at the many faces. I was sure that everyone was looking at me with sympathy and pity.

"He needs to go to jail! His ass needs to rot in jail! You need to press charges."

"No."

"No?" I heard my cousin Roxanne ask.

"No. I'm not pressing charges. I'm not going to court. I'm not testifying. I'm not telling a courtroom what he did to me that night. Just no."

"Savannah you have to. Livy died to tell the truth. She died for you."

"She didn't die for me. She died because of me."

"What do you mean?"

"I..."

My loud sobs filled the room. I cried from a place that was broken; from a place that was empty.

"What do you mean?"

I shook my head. "She didn't do it for me."

I could feel how tensed Jace's body was next to me. He had to be angry. To hear that a man that he'd loved and respected, his friend, had raped me had to make him angry. But he hadn't said anything.

I buried my face in his chest and continued to release my pain.

"Savannah?"

I looked up at the sound of his voice.

It was Kori.

"I'm sorry for your loss."

I didn't say anything.

"I came by to see if it was any truth to what Livy had said. And to see if you wanted to press charges, if so."

"Hell yeah!" Grandma shouted.

Kori waited on my answer.

He looked sympathetic, just like everyone else.

Did I want to press charges?

Would it even matter if I did?

The damage was already done, and the truth was finally out.

I didn't have to hide it anymore. I was free.

"No."

Grandma started to curse.

"No?"

"No," I repeated.

Kori nodded. "Well, if you ever change your mind you know where to find me," Kori said. He started to leave.

"Wait."

He turned to face me.

"When you, or the detective, question Harvey about mama, ask him what he said to me on prom night."

"What did he say?"

The whole room seemed to be awaiting my response.

"He said...he said...just ask him."

Kori didn't pressure me to say anything else. He just nodded his head.

As soon as he walked out of the house, everyone started to ask me questions all at once.

There was so much noise, and so much chatter, that I couldn't hear myself think. I looked at Jace.

"Jace?"

"Yeah."

"Get me out of here please."

Jace stood up, and then he picked me up. He held me in his arms, walked past my family and out the front door. He put me into his truck and with my whole family now on the front porch, he drove away.

We drove in silence for a long time.

"Is there anything you want to ask me?"

"No."

"Do you want to know what happened?"

Jace was upset. I could tell by the way he was breathing and the way he flared his nose.

"You can tell me whenever you're ready. If you are ever ready."

We were both silent, again, until he decided to ask a question. "That's why you left isn't it?"

I looked over at him. "Yes. A big part of it."

He didn't ask me anything else.

We arrived at his house, and Jace asked me what I needed.

I told him that I didn't need anything.

I just wanted to lay there. I just wanted to cry.

And so, for hours, that's exactly what I did.

I laid. I cried. And Jace never left my side.

~***~

"I need you to tell me the comment that Mr. Harvey Woods made."

Kori must've told Detective Brent what I'd said.

With the rape out in the open, there was no point in keeping the comment to myself. Maybe it could help with the investigation.

"He said that if I told anyone, about what he did to me, I would end up dead like my mother."

The detective wrote down my comment.

"So, he did rape you?"

"Yes. But I'm not pressing charges, and I'm not going to court."

Detective Brent nodded his head.

"He probably did it. Right? He was obsessed with mama, and he made that comment. He probably killed her."

"Well, he has an alibi for that night. Upon checking into him, I'd gone to see a few men that worked for him back in the day. I asked generic questions. I asked them where they were when they heard about the murder. I didn't point the finger at Harvey. I just asked. And then I asked where they'd been the night that your mother was killed. All of them said that they were at the barbershop until about nine; including Harvey. And from there they said they went to a bar to have drinks. They were there for most of the night. They said that Harvey got so drunk that he had to be driven home."

I rolled my eyes.

"So, unless he faked being drunk, went back out that night, after being dropped off, and killed your mother...most likely, he didn't do it."

I didn't say anything.

"But..."

My heart skipped a beat.

"Your mother and father were in fact still seeing each other often. His wife thinks romantically, although he denies that part. Mr. Hosea, the owner of the little convenience store that's been across from the hardware store, for years, told me that a few weeks before your mother's murder, he saw the three of them outside of the store arguing. Frank, his wife, and your mother. He wasn't sure why, but he said your mother yelled for a while, before getting into her car and driving away. After she was gone, Dora, Frank's wife, slapped him, yelled at him, and then she drove away too. Mr. Hosea was never questioned back then either."

Wow!

What were they arguing about?

"I can't put my finger on it, but the wife seems like she's hiding something. Your father just seems like he's hiding the whole truth about their affair. They have the same alibi for that night; one that can't be verified by a third party. They both said that they were home in bed...together. That may be the truth. Or it could be a lie. But we're still looking. There were a lot of things missed the first time around. I plan to look into all of them. I'm going to find out the truth. That's the least I can do for you."

After he said a few more words, he was gone.

Cassy came outside.

She looked at me, with a judgmental expression and silently, I prayed that she didn't say the wrong thing to me.

Today just wasn't the day for her smart-ass mouth, and as God is my witness, she had one time to say something out the way to me, and I was going to give her ass a *two-piece* and a biscuit!

"How are you?"

"I'm fine," I answered her.

She sat down next to me. She zipped up her jacket, and then she spoke again. "I know how it feels to be ashamed of something."

Here we go.

"I'm not good at sex."

Accidentally, I laughed.

"It's not the same as what you went through. It's not as bad. But I know how it feels to be ashamed, and to want to hide your truth. Truth is, I knew that it was only a matter of time before my husband cheated on me. Every man that I've ever been with has. And it's because I have horrible sex."

"What do you mean?"

"I mean everything I do is wrong. It seems awkward or off. I've watched porn so many times, but when it comes time to do "it"...I'm horrible. So, most of the time I just lay there like a dead dog and let them do whatever they are going to do."

I laughed so hard.

And from a good healthy place too.

Cassy cracked a smile.

"Girl, don't ask me why Corbin wanted to marry me. I was surprised. I don't suck dick or anything. Every time that I try too, it's always an epic fail. I'm just sexually awkward. It's like I don't know how to be sexy or anything. And I was too ashamed to ask for pointers or help. Lord knows, I wanted to ask Marlo's nasty self so many times, but I thought that she would laugh."

As much as I love Marlo, I wanted to tell Cassy the truth so bad.

"Are you serious about this? Or are you just trying to cheer me up?"

"Oh no, I'm dead ass serious."

"Well...I can teach you some stuff."

"Really?"

"Yes. Only if you agree to go home tonight and try them with Corbin. I know things are bad between y'all, after what he did, but I can tell that you still love him. I can tell that you're going to forgive him. Eventually. Even though he doesn't deserve it. No one can judge you if you do. Just don't let him do that to you again...if you decide to go back. But I can teach you a thing or two. Then you can go and try them with Corbin. Tonight. I'll even watch the baby."

Cassy grinned. "We've never really gotten along, have we?"

"No. Not really."

"I'm sorry for what happened to you."

"Thank you. Now I wonder if grandma has some pickles! The first lesson is learning to suck some dick! Chile, there's power in sucking a mean one. Trust me...ask me how I passed a class that I was failing in college with an A+. It's all about the throat baby. It's all about the throat."

We both chuckled as we headed indoors.

As promised, I spent a while giving Cassy pointers, and then she was off to try and fix her marriage.

I sat on the couch with the baby.

I should've given Nathaniel babies. I was getting older now, and I felt as though I was running out of time.

I wished that I hadn't been so selfish.

Nathaniel.

He didn't know anything about what had gone on, and every time that I spoke to him, I didn't mention it. He still didn't know the truth about what Harvey did to me.

As of right now, he was the only one not talking to me like I was a victim. He was the only one treating me like I was normal. Even though Jace tried to be normal, he was all over me. He was checking on me every five seconds and everything else in between.

I played with the baby a little, and then I got her ready for bed. I bathed her, fed her and then I rocked her to sleep.

Once she was asleep, I walked over to the table preparing to open my laptop and write, but instead, I had this urge to journal. I went into my bag to get my journal, but then I remembered that I had Gamma's, so I pulled out hers instead.

I curled up in the bed beside the baby, and I read the first page.

The first entry was from September 16th, 2002.

She talked about the death of one of my great aunts; one of her kids. She journaled about the funeral, and how she felt seeing her for last time. She recalled why she'd named her Joanne and called her a miracle baby.

The next entry wasn't until June 2003.

She was mad at Grandma Whinny. She called her name after name, and she said that she was stupid for staying with grandpa. Gamma obviously knew about grandpa's affair and she even referenced what she'd gone through with her own husband.

I read a few more entries, and at some time or another, I must've fallen asleep. I woke up to the sound of the bedroom door creaking open.

It was Cassy.

"Hey. So, how did it go?" I asked her, wiping my eyes.

She didn't say anything.

"Cassy."

A small lamp was turned on in the far corner of the room, so I couldn't really see Cassy's face, but I could hear her breathing.

"Cassy? What's wrong?"

"I stopped for a drink once I got on that side of town. I needed to loosen up a little. I needed to calm my nerves. I had two drinks, and then I headed towards the house. I was ready. I was excited. I was going to walk into the house and just give myself to him. I wasn't going to ask about the mistress or anything. I was just going to try and please him. If it was just this one time, I was going to try."

Her voice started to crack, so I sat up.

"Both of Corbin's cars were in our driveway. Just his. But he wasn't in the house alone. As soon as I opened the front door, I could hear the sounds."

No. No. No!

"I could hear him. And I could hear her."

Oh my God!

Cassy caught Marlo and Corbin having sex!

"I was furious! I wanted to see who she was. I wanted to see the bitch that had taken my husband from me. I tip-toed down the hall, but not before grabbing Corbin's wooden bat out of the hallway closet. I didn't really plan on using it. I was just going to scare them, I guess. There was so much noise. She was screaming, and he was moaning. They were so loud. I could hear the headboard slamming up against the wall. Corbin was telling her how good her pussy was and..." Cassy paused. "And then he told her that he loved her. I guess hearing him say those words to another woman just...I just snapped!"

I got all the way out of the bed and walked past Cassy to turn on the room light. Immediately, I placed my hands over my mouth.

There were a few splats of blood on her face, shirt and hands.

"She was riding his dick, and then...she wasn't. I hit her in the back of the head with the bat. I think...I think she's dead."

"Cassy no! Oh no! Please tell me you didn't! Please tell me you didn't kill Marlo! Please!"

My heart ached, but her next statement caught me by surprise.

"Marlo? Who said anything about Marlo? Why would you think I killed Marlo?"

Huh?

Oh shit! How was I going to get out of this one?

"Why would you think I was talking about Marlo? It wasn't Marlo that was fucking my husband. It was Jace's ex-wife. Reeva."

"What!"

"I didn't know it was her until she was lying on the bed, bleeding from the back of her head."

Emotions hit me like a 5.5 earthquake, and I had to take a seat.

What was Jace's ex-wife doing with Corbin?

She was engaged. What was she doing there?

"I was hysterical. I was scared. I didn't mean to, I was just so angry. Corbin shouted, and I just stood there. I couldn't move. I couldn't do anything. Surprisingly, Corbin didn't fuss at me. Instead, he started to shake me. Corbin told me to leave, after he apologized for cheating on me and causing something like this to happen. He told me to go, and not to tell anyone that I was there. He told me to keep it a secret. Corbin said that our daughter needs me, and that he would take the blame. He just wanted me to go."

A lot of things were on my mind.

I was thinking about Jace. I was thinking about his daughter and that she'd probably just lost her mother. I was thinking about Cassy and Corbin. And I was thinking about...

"Marlo. Marlo slept with my husband? Didn't she? And she told you? You knew?"

"No...Yes...No. Cassy, I told her that it was wrong. I thought you killed her. I didn't mean to..."

"You didn't mean to tell me that my cousin is a tramp! I can't believe this. I can't believe her! And I can't believe you!" Cassy screamed. She placed her hands on her head. "Oh, you just wait until I tell Luis! As a matter of fact, I'm going over there right now! I'm going to tell him and then as for Marlo... "

Cassy turned around.

"No! The blood. You have blood on you, Cassy."

She froze.

"You have Reeva's blood on you. On your clothes and on your face. And what about your daughter? If Corbin takes the blame, she's going to lose her father tonight. For you, he's about to go to prison. Probably forever. Your daughter needs you. She needs you."

Cassy turned back around to face me.

She was crying.

I wanted to hug her, but I didn't.

"Go wash up. And come back and get your daughter," I said to her. "Please. Just stay here with your daughter tonight."

Finally, Cassy nodded her head, and then she disappeared.

I broke down as soon as she was out of sight.

This was bad!

Corbin was sleeping with Reeva.

Cassy killed her...maybe.

Corbin was taking the blame.

I accidentally told on Marlo.

And now Cassy was going to ruin her marriage too.

And I had no idea how Jace was going to feel about this. I didn't know how he was going to react.

Not knowing what to do, I just sat there and did nothing.

I sat there until Cassy came back into the room.

And together, we both just sat there.

And together, we cried, without saying one single word.

"What the hell happened?"

Grandma screamed at the T.V. as they showed Corbin in handcuffs the next morning.

I wondered what Corbin was going to tell them.

How would he explain what happened?

The news reporter said that he wasn't speaking to anyone, and that they were taking him in for questioning. The reporter said that Corbin had called 9-1-1 that night and asked for help, but that was all they knew. He was refusing to talk to anyone without his lawyer present.

I glanced at Cassy.

She was shaking, so I touched her leg.

The news reporter also said that the woman hadn't died, as of yet, and that Reeva was still alive. She was in the hospital fighting for her life. If Reeva lived, she was going to tell the truth. She was going to tell the cops that it wasn't Corbin who attacked her. And eventually, Cassy was going to go to jail.

I'd tried to call Jace, but his phone was going straight to voicemail. Any other day, he would've called me a hundred times by now, or answered my call on the first ring, but today, so far, I hadn't been able to reach him.

"I can't believe this shit! And Corbin was cheating with Jayceon's ex-wife? Damn. I hate that. I really hate that. Cassy, I'm sorry baby," grandma huffed. Cassy didn't say anything.

"Cassy? Cassy? Are you okay?" My cousins Eve and Roxanne came into the house together. They immediately tried to comfort their sister. Cassy didn't say a word.

Seconds later, in walked Marlo and Luis.

"Cassy, we heard the news. I'm so sorry," Marlo said.

I'd been calling her all morning too, but she hadn't answered her phone. I'd texted her that we needed to talk, but I didn't want to say anything specific in the text message just in case Luis had access to her phone.

"Get her away from me," Cassy growled.

Everyone looked at Marlo.

"Cassy, what's wrong?" Eve asked her.

"It should've been her!"

I tried to calm Cassy down, but it wasn't working.

"Marlo has been sleeping with my husband too!"

"I know you betta' be lying!" Grandma proclaimed, although I was sure that she wasn't surprised. It just confirmed what she'd already assumed.

"You fucked my husband!"

Cassy was now on her feet. She shoved Marlo, sending her flying back into her husband's arms.

"What? What are you talking about?"

"Don't deny it!"

Cassy attempted to grab Marlo's hair, but Eve grabbed her hand.

"Savannah slipped up."

Marlo looked at me.

"I'm sorry. I didn't mean to say it. I thought…it slipped."

"She thought I…I mean, she thought Corbin killed you. Well, Reeva's not dead, but still, she thought it was you! It should've been you!"

Marlo was still looking at me.

"I didn't know. I'm sorry. I didn't mean to say it."

"So, it's true?" Marlo's husband, Luis spoke.

It was as though everyone else had forgotten that he was there until he opened his mouth.

"Look at me, Marlo."

She didn't. She continued to look at me.

"Marlo? Is it true?"

She took a deep breath. "Yes."

Cassy cursed and reached for Marlo's hair again. This time she got it and pulled Marlo towards her. Marlo swung her fist, connected with Cassy's jaw. Cassy let her hair go.

Luis started to back away from Marlo. "So, the baby that you're carrying. That you just found out you're pregnant with. Is it mine?"

Marlo was breathing hard.

Marlo is pregnant? Again?

"No," Marlo confessed.

Cassy lost it, and they had to lie on top of her to keep her from getting to Marlo.

Luis dropped his head, and then he turned around. He punched a hole in the wall on his way out the front door. He slammed the door so hard the whole house seemed to shake.

"You should've never come here," Marlo said to me.

"What?"

"You heard me. It's been nothing but death and chaos since you got here. You should've never come back here."

"Oh no, don't blame your shit on me! I told you to stop sleeping with your cousin's husband! It's not my fault that you got caught!"

"Actually Savannah, it is. I didn't get caught. You told."

Marlo stormed out of the house.

I noticed that grandma had just been sitting there. As though she was going to wait and see how it all played out.

"How long was she sleeping with Corbin?"

"I don't know."

"How could you know something like that and not tell her? If it were your husband, you would've wanted to know!" Eve said. "Wait, I forgot. You don't have a husband. He left you!"

208

"It wasn't my place to tell her! It wasn't my business! I told Marlo she was wrong. She's a grown ass woman! I couldn't stop her from doing what she wanted to do!"

"You could've tried," Roxanne commented.

They helped Cassy up and ushered her towards the door. She looked back at me as though she wanted me to realize that it was them and not her who was still upset with me.

She knew I knew the truth.

She knew that I knew her secret.

Whether or not she thought I owed her to keep it or not.

The ladies disappeared, and then it was just grandma and me.

"I knew it was one of them. I didn't know which one, but I knew it was one of them."

"It's not my fault. I hadn't meant to say anything."

"It was bound to come out sooner or later. Everything always does. Even those little things that we don't want people to know. Somehow, they end up knowing them anyway. She'll get over it. They'll get over it. That's Marlo's and Corbin's sin. Not yours. Have you spoken to Jayceon yet?"

"No. He's not picking up the phone."

"One big mess, I tell you. One big mess."

Grandma started to hum and pray.

Without telling her where I was going, I grabbed my car keys and headed out the door. Jayceon had long since taken my windshield to get fixed, although I hadn't driven my car in what seemed like forever.

Surprisingly, once I got outside, all of the ladies were still there. Cassy, Roxanne and Eve were on the front porch. Marlo was sitting in grandma's car. Her husband had left.

I didn't bother trying to speak my peace. And none of them said anything to me either. I got into my car, and I hit the gas. I had no idea where I was going.

Everything was a mess.

And things were far from being over.

Livy's memorial service was tomorrow.

I wasn't sure how Jace was feeling.

Corbin was going to go to jail for something that he didn't do, and I wasn't sure how I felt about knowing the truth. I hadn't asked to have to carry the weight of yet another secret; and of all people, Cassy's secret. But I couldn't turn her in. I would never do that.

Surprisingly, my car stopped in front of the hardware store. I wasn't sure why I was there, but it's where my heart led me. Barely thinking things through, I waltzed into the store. I didn't see him, Frank, so I asked the cashier if he was there. The employee told me that he was in his office. I found the office in the back of the store, and I walked right in.

"We both know that you're my dad. What I want to know is why you don't love me? Why didn't you want me?"

For as long as I could remember, I'd always wanted to know the answers to those questions. And he was going to answer them. Damn it! He was going to answer me!

He looked at me and then he sat down his pen.

"Hello, Savannah."

Hearing him say my name made me feel sad.

"You want the truth. Okay. I'll give it to you. The truth is, I let my wife dictate my role in your life and I shouldn't have."

"So, you wanted to be there?"

I sounded like a sad little girl.

"I did. Believe it or not, I loved your mother. Glorianne was special."

"I bet you say that to all your mistresses! You lied to her."

"Yes. I did. Dora and I hadn't been happy for years when I met your mother, but Dora's family had the money. They helped me open the stores. They are part owners. It was just so much that played a role in the decisions that I made."

I could tell by the look on his face that he was reflecting, regretting, and wishing that he'd done things differently.

"When I found out your mother was pregnant, I thought about giving it all up. I knew I would have to if I wanted to be with her. The store was just starting out. Without Dora's families' help and money, it would've failed. But I'd thought about it. I really did."

My father leaned back in his chair.

"And then your mother found out. She found out before I was ready to tell her. Before I could make up my mind. And before I could decide on what I really wanted to do. She found out that I was married. Glorianne told me that she didn't want anything to do with me. She told me that she would raise you on her own. And then my wife told me that if I wanted to keep my business, then I would let her. She told me to cut all ties with Glorianne, and that she would never accept you. I had to choose."

I exhaled loudly, anticipating his next words.

"I tried to see if your mother would want me. I tried to see if she would forgive me and want to be a family, but she wouldn't talk to me. All she ever said was to leave her alone and not to worry about you. So, I stayed. I stayed married. I stayed with Dora. And I gave her what she wanted. I agreed not to see Glorianne and that I wouldn't bring you around. You're your mother changed her mind. Eventually, she came around. But it was too late."

He opened his desk drawer.

He pulled out a stack of photos. They were of me. Some of the photos were from as far back as the age of one.

"She came here one day, months after you were born, and asked me if I still felt the same. I did. But things had changed. Dora was now pregnant with my son. I couldn't just choose her anymore. It wasn't that simple anymore. I had a son coming."

"And you had a daughter," I growled.

"Yes. I did. Glorianne understood. She asked what I wanted to do about you. I talked to my wife again, but she still refused to have anything to do with you. She said that we were about to have a son and that we had our own family. And that you couldn't be a part of it. I told Glorianne. I tried to find a solution. I told her that I would come and see you and that she could bring you by the store, but that my wife wouldn't allow you in our home. It was her who said that if my wife couldn't accept you, then I couldn't see you. She made that decision. She said that she wasn't going to allow me to make you a secret. She said that she wouldn't let me do to you, what I'd done to her. She said that it wouldn't be fair to you. And I allowed it. To keep my wife happy, I allowed your mother to keep you away from me."

I wanted to cry, but I didn't.

"Glorianne hated her decision though. She would bring me pictures of you. I'm not sure if it was to remind me of what I was missing out on or because she felt sorry for me. She always brought me pictures. I always looked at them. You remind me of your mother. I loved her. It was like this forbidden love. As though you are looking at something on display and you can see it, but you can't touch it. She would come in here, and give me pictures of you, and then just stare at me. Sometimes, she didn't want to talk at all. She would just stare. For years, she wouldn't take my money. Giving her money was the least I could do. Even if she wouldn't let me see you, I could help take care of you. Once you got older, she started to take some of the money, every now and then, but never too much. She would always give some of it back. I don't know why. And then when she died..."

He pulled the clipping of the newspaper out of his desk.

"I wish I would've chosen differently. I wish I would've chosen her. I wasn't in love with my wife. I should've left Dora. Glorianne still loved me. She was just upset because I lied. I should've tried harder. And I should've been there for you. No matter what it would've cost me. I should've been there."

This was the truth straight from the horse's mouth.

"Why were you arguing? Outside? With your wife and mama?"

"Oh, that day, Dora popped up at the store. Glorianne was here. We never had sex after the truth came out. Never. But when Dora caught us talking in my office, she thought that we were still fooling around. Things got heated, and I followed Glorianne out of the store. Dora was upset. She was upset that I was still talking to her and that I was seeing her. She was convinced that we were still having an affair. We weren't. When your mother drove away that day, I never saw her again. She never came back to the store, and that was the last time I saw her alive."

He stared at the newspaper clipping. "I came to the funeral. I sat way in the back of the church. I didn't walk around the casket. I just sat there. I saw you in the front. You were crying, and I wished that I could've comforted you. I loved your mother. I really did. And I loved you. I still do."

I stared at him.

"After she died, I wondered if I should introduce myself to you. You were older. I no longer cared what Dora would have to say. I wanted to know you, but I convinced myself that you were better off without me."

I could tell that his words were sincere.

I didn't like them, and I didn't like that no one thought about me or how I would feel, as a result of their choices, but I could tell that his words were the truth. I could tell that he was being honest.

"You didn't kill her, did you?"

"No. I would never."

"And your wife…would she have killed her?"

"I guess you can never be sure of what someone might do. As I told the police, I remember going home early that night and going to bed. When I fell asleep, she was there. That's all I know."

"Why did you lie when I asked you if you were my dad?"

"Honestly, I wasn't sure what to say." My father stood up and reached out his hand. "Hello, I'm Frank Jones. I'm your father."

I stared at his hand for a few seconds. I tried to sort out my feelings. I tried to figure out if I was angry or hurt by the truth. I concluded that I was both, but it was time to move on. It was time for closure. So, after exhaling, I shook his hand. "Hi Frank, I'm Savannah Lynch. I'm your daughter."

~***~

None of my family, other than grandma was there.

Livy's memorial was short and sweet. A few of her family members came. Some said they hadn't seen Livy in so long that they didn't see the point in showing up to pay their respects.

No one else wanted Livy's ashes, so I took them with me. No one even bothered to cook or prepare a place to gather after the service. Everyone just went home.

"I'll see you later grandma. I'm going to the hospital."

"How is she doing?"

"I'm not sure. I talked to Jace for all of five minutes yesterday, so I'm going to go up there and check on him."

I reached her the urn.

"I guess just put it up."

She nodded.

I drove to the hospital in silence.

After finding out what floor Jace's ex-wife was on, I made my way to Jace. I couldn't help but wonder if I was overstepping my boundaries.

As I approached, I saw Jace, his mother and father, his daughter, one of his buddies, and I assumed some of Reeva's family, in a small waiting area.

"Well, what a surprise. I didn't know you were still in town," Jace's mother, Sharon replied.

She stood up to greet me.

Jace's father, the Pastor, embraced me next.

Finally, Jace stood up from sitting next to his daughter and walked in my direction.

We stepped away.

"Hey."

"Hey."

"I was going to call."

Jace dropped his head.

"Hey. Hey. It's going be okay."

I'd never ever seen him cry. I was almost in disbelief of the wetness on my thumbs as I wiped his eyes.

"Everything is going to be okay."

I stood on my tip-toes as Jace came down to my level and placed his forehead against mine. We stood there for a while. As though there wasn't anyone else around.

"Jace?" His mother called his name.

We both looked in her direction. She was smiling at us in approval, but then her smile turned into a frown once Jace noticed the doctor.

"I regret to inform you…"

~***~

Note to self: Leave this awful place and never come back.

No one was speaking to me, except for grandma. Apparently, no one liked that fact that I'd kept Marlo's secret.

Marlo hadn't even bothered to come back around.

I'd overheard Tatianna telling grandma that Luis left her and that she wasn't doing too good.

Cassy wasn't doing well either.

She was sick with guilt and heartache.

No one still knew much about what Corbin was saying, but at least if he took the blame, he wouldn't be going to jail for murder.

The doctor came out to tell Jace that Reeva had woken up from her coma. She was alive, but she'd suffered severe head trauma. Not only did she not remember anything or anyone, but she could no longer speak, she was blind in one eye, and she was paralyzed from the neck down.

They called it a miracle; only I wasn't sure if it should be seen as such. Reeva's life, as she knew it, was over. I wondered if she even thought it was worth living.

Jace wasn't himself. He was worried about her. He was worried about their daughter. Her mother didn't even remember her. Jace said that his daughter wouldn't leave her mother's side.

I was trying to give him some space, and room to be there for his child. So, I was stuck at the plantation house, feeling invisible and out of place.

"Everything is gonna' be alright, baby," Grandma Whinny touched my shoulder.

It was Sunday.

Everyone was gathered there as usual. Grandma had found me sitting outside in the cold all alone.

"You know, no one has seen "Nasty Harvey" since the truth came out."

"Maybe he left town."

"I reckon so," she said. "I wished I'd been able to put my hands around his throat before he left.

I didn't say anything.

"You and Marlo will make up. Cassy and Marlo will make up. Everything will be fine."

"Grandma…"

I paused.

Running my mouth was what got me into the predicament I was in now. That's why no one wanted to talk to me. But I had to say something. I had to get this burden off of me.

"Grandma…Cassy…"

"I know."

I looked at her.

"She told me. Now, only Corbin, Cassy, us and the Good Lord knows the truth. He owes her this. He caused this. He deserves this. He should take the blame for this."

I exhaled.

I hated to think that Reeva deserved what happened to her. She was in the wrong, absolutely, but I couldn't say that she deserved to suffer the way that she was.

"Marlo will get hers as well. What goes around always comes right back around. And most of the time, it circles around twice. From what I hear, it's already startin'. She lost the baby. Luis is keepin' the kids, and he wants her out of the house. I assume she'll be movin' in over here. I'll whip her back into shape after I curse her ass out a few times! Then, I'll help her heal. Her and Cassy both."

Grandma paused. "And you."

I didn't need healing.

I needed…

217

Honestly, I wasn't sure.

We both stared at the police car as it came down the long driveway. Soon, my brother, the sheriff, got out of the car and strutted towards me.

"Hello, ladies."

Grandma nodded.

"How are you holding…"

"I'll be fine. Something new with the case?"

Kori placed his thumbs inside of his pockets.

"Actually, yes. I wanted to be the first to tell you. We've had another development, and I'm not sure how you're going to feel about it."

"This isn't about my feelings. This is about the truth. Just tell me."

"Well, I wanted you to know that Grice Hall is being brought in for questioning."

"Grice Hall" Grandma spoke up.

"What? Why?"

"He's come up in the investigation. As it turns out, your mother wasn't having an affair with *our* father. She had one with Grice."

I started to shake my head.

"No. That's a mistake. That can't be true."

"It is. He already confirmed it."

My mouth opened wide, as grandma started to curse out of the blue.

Grice Hall was the Pastor.

And my soon-to-be father-in-law too.

****

CHAPTER EIGHT

This is where they found her.

Since I've been back, I'd avoided coming here, but now I was ready.

I got out of my car and stood in front of the field.

There were traces of cotton left behind signaling that the field had recently been harvested.

It was cold, windy, early evening, but since time had gone back, the sun was already about to go down.

Still, I made my way through the field. I headed to the exact spot where they found her body.

I was surprised to see that there weren't any signs of the police being there. Since they'd found new evidence, I'd assumed that they had found it there and that there would be some kind of yellow tape nearby, but there wasn't any.

Maybe they'd found the new evidence somewhere else.

Her murder obviously hadn't stopped the owners of the land from producing. It was as though her death hadn't mattered. As though no one really cared.

But I cared.

I cared then.

And even after finding out all of her secrets and bad decisions, I cared now.

Mama was sleeping with Jace's father, Pastor Hall.

Eww!

Mama's car had been spotted in the church's parking lot the night that she died. I remember the mention of it back then, but it was said that she was only in the parking lot for a few minutes. And then drove away. The police left it at that. But the new detective asked the right questions. Apparently, a *few* minutes was more like twenty. She'd sat in the parking lot for about twenty-minutes that night, with her car running.

Why?

Back then, Pastor Hall had only been questioned as to why she could've been at the church that night. He told them that he was unsure. On record, he stated that maybe she'd been waiting for someone or that she could've pulled in because she was tired. The factory where Mama worked was right down the street from the church. After working long hours, it wouldn't have been the first time a member pulled into the church's parking lot for a cat nap.

The Pastor wasn't asked anything else. No one ever suspected that he was involved with my mother, but he hadn't been able to fool Detective Brent.

Detective Brent had gone to speak to Jace's parents about my mother and that night; after he had already talked to the gentleman that had seen her in the church's parking lot fifteen years ago. He asked Pastor Hall the same questions he'd been asked before, only this time, he asked him where he was that night.

Jace's father answered that he was home, but Jace's mother reminded him that he'd gone out for a while. She remembered that he'd gone down to the jail to see if he could help a member of the church post bail for their son. She remembered because it was homecoming night, and she'd stayed behind only to make sure that Jace made it home safely.

Detective Brent looked into Jace's father's story.

He'd lied.

He never went down to the jail that night.

So, he met with Pastor Hall, again, alone, and asked him where he was. This time, he told him that he'd been on his way to the church that night, but that he'd changed his mind. He said he drove around for a little while, and then he'd gone back home.

I'm not sure what happened after that or what the detective told him that convinced him to come clean about his affair with mama, but after being taken to the jail for questioning, finally, he admitted the truth.

Jace's father, Pastor Grice Hall of Living Rock and Holy Waters A.M.E. Zion Church, had been sleeping with my mother.

He told the detective that they'd been meeting up at the church for only a few weeks; usually when she got off work. He said that it would've been their fifth time having sex, at the church, but he didn't show up. He said that the lies were starting to take a toll on him. He said that he felt convicted and that he stood her up.

Did he really?

I was speechless.

Not only was he fooling around with mama, but he was screwing her at the church?

Both of them should be ashamed!

Well, she was dead, but I sure hope she'd prayed and asked for forgiveness.

Pastor Hall said she'd come to talk to him one night about her problems and her drinking. He said they started to cry and while he was comforting her, something happened. They kissed. And then one thing led to another.

The town was going to have a field day with this discovery, once it got out. If it got out. For now, it hadn't.

Pastor Hall didn't have an airtight alibi for where he was for that short period of time. The first lady couldn't be sure of when he came home because she said that she'd fallen asleep. He told the detective the names of the roads he traveled, but it would take some digging to see if any of it could be proven; especially fifteen years later.

It had been a day and a half since Kori told me about the affair, but I hadn't spoken to Jace about it yet. I could barely get him on the phone. I wasn't even sure if he'd heard. All I kept thinking about was how I would feel and how it would affect my feelings for Jace if it came back that his father was a murderer.

If his father killed my mother.

Standing in the field, I stared at the spot where someone had dumped her body as though she was nothing. She'd been fully dressed. A single blow to her head. I wished she'd been a miracle like Reeva. She'd been out here for hours before she was found. Maybe if she'd been taken to the hospital, maybe she would've lived.

Briefly, I remembered how she looked on the day of her funeral. She was beautiful. I remembered thinking that for the first time, ever, she looked at peace. She never looked that way before, when she was alive. She always looked so stressed and unhappy. Maybe even a little depressed. She died too young, and way before her time. And all I wanted was for her killer to do the time, for the crime. No matter who it is. And no matter what she'd done. She didn't deserve to die.

I shivered from the strokes of the wind, but I didn't walk away. I continued to stand there. So much has happened since I've been here. Both bad and good. This was the last thing. Finding out the truth about what happened to mama was all that was missing.

The sudden crunching noises behind me caused my heart to drop. Hurriedly, I turned around.

Harvey.

My chest tightened with fear.

The sun had gone down, and instantly, I regretted coming out here alone.

"Hello, Savannah."

I didn't speak.

I looked past him towards my car. He'd parked his right in front of mine. I'd been so consumed with my thoughts that I hadn't been paying attention. I hadn't heard him pull up.

"What are you doing out here? A pretty girl like yourself shouldn't be out here alone."

Since no one had seen or heard from him, I thought that he was long gone. I thought that he'd left town, gone somewhere to hide, afraid that I was going to share my story and put his perverted ass in jail.

"It's a little chilly out here tonight. Come here."

I didn't move.

I noticed that he had his left arm in a sling; as a result of the gunshot wound.

The wind whistled as though it was telling me to make a run for it. I had the advantage.

He only has one good arm.

I wasn't as young as I was before. I could fight back.

Then why was I so afraid?

"Come here, Savannah. Gimme' kiss," Harvey taunted me.

Harvey was grinning. It was the same evil smirk from prom night. The one that he'd had before doing his dirty deed.

I took my first step.

Harvey stepped in the same direction.

"Uh uh, where you goin'?"

"Move Harvey."

"And what if I don't?"

I took another step.

He took one too.

It was getting darker and darker by the second, and I was trying not to panic. We were on an old country road about five minutes out of city limits. It was nothing but fields. The closest house was roughly a mile away.

"Tell me that you didn't enjoy that night. I know I did."

Harvey stepped towards me, and I decided right then and there that I wasn't going to be a victim of his again.

With my heart racing, I watched him watching me. The sound of what sounded like a car coming down the road caused him to look behind him and with the sight of the headlights...

Now!

It all happened so fast.

One moment I was running and the next...I wasn't.

Harvey had pushed me from behind, and I went tumbling to the ground.

"Where do you think you're going, huh?"

Immediately, I regretted not pressing charges on him. He would be locked up, right now, if I had.

Frantically, I turned over onto my back, and I tried to get back on my feet. Harvey kicked me down.

"You know you want me."

"Get away from me!"

He growled. "Oh, so Jace is good enough for some pussy, but I ain't?"

In the dark, I patted the ground. Maybe there was something nearby that I could use to protect myself.

"When I saw you drive past me, in your fancy car, I knew you were coming down here. So, I followed you. There's no one here to save you. Just like that night. No one can save you. Just give me what I want, and you can go home."

Harvey inched closer to me, as I tried to back away from him.

"Give it to me!"

"No!"

He leaned over and tried to grab me by the leg. I kicked at his arm, the one that was in the sling.

"No!"

"Well, I'm just going to have to take it again."

Harvey tried to grab my leg again using his one good arm and hand, but I wouldn't stop kicking.

"Stop it! Stop it!"

I grabbed for whatever was underneath my hand, and I threw what felt like dirt and rocks in his face.

"You bitch!" Harvey growled. "I'm going to fuck you. And then I'm going to kill you!"

Kill me?

His words caused me to space out for a second too long, and by the time I came back to reality, Harvey was holding my leg.

He started to drag me closer to him.

I started to scream at the top of my lungs.

"No! No! N---"

BANG!

The sudden sound almost caused me to urinate on myself. My mouth was still wide open as Harvey dropped my leg. I hurried away from him, and just as I stood to my feet, Harvey fell to the ground.

And then I saw him.

Kori.

My brother.

"Are you okay?"

He was still holding the gun.

I didn't answer him.

Harvey wasn't moving.

"Are you okay?" He repeated.

"Yeah. Yeah. I think so."

Kori kicked Harvey's leg. He's dead.

Thank goodness! Finally, he's dead!

"Go on. I'll take care of this. Get out of here."

I tried to figure out what I wanted to say.

"I drove by. My folk's house is about another mile up the road. I noticed your car. You're the only person with a car like that around here. It wasn't until I was a quarter of a mile up the road that it hit me. I realized that the other car was Harvey's. And then I remembered what Livy said that day. And what she said he did to you. So, I turned around. I'm glad I did."

"He was going to rape me. He was going to kill me," I mumbled. "You killed him."

"Someone had to. Go. I'll figure this out."

"No. Thank you. But I can stay. I'll say whatever I need to say to make sure that you don't go down for this. You saved me. You saved my life."

Kori nodded, and then called for backup.

In no time, the scene became flooded with police, medical experts and media.

I gave my statements, and I added in a little extra to make sure that Kori was covered.

We both told the same story.

I was out there alone, mourning my mother's death. Harvey followed me. He tried to rape me. Kori was passing by and spotted our cars. He heard my screams. And then, he approached the situation and warned Harvey to stop. He saw Harvey raise a hand to me as though he was about to harm me, and after another verbal warning, he shot him.

No, that wasn't exactly how it happened. We embellished the truth just a little, but we'd wanted to make sure that the shot was "clean". Even though

Kori felt as though he'd done the right thing, it was my idea to add in a few details.

No one ever had to know the whole truth.

Our first brother-sister secret.

After all was said and done, Kori ushered me to my car. "Thank you again, for tonight. Thank you for saving me from Harvey."

"He deserved it."

He sure did.

I shut my car door and then rolled down my driver's side window.

"Can I ask you something?"

"Sure."

What new evidence was found to reopen my mother's case?"

Kori checked his surroundings. "There wasn't any."

"What?"

"I 'made' evidence just to have the case reopened. There wasn't any."

"Why would you do that?"

"I was kind of hoping that it was him."

"Who?"

"Our father. After I discovered your mother had been murdered and that the case was unsolved, I made it my business to check into it. I was angry, and after reading over the case, I wondered if he was guilty of the crime. I wanted him to be guilty. I'd worked hard all of my life not to disappoint him. I didn't want to live off their money. I wanted to make my own way. I wanted him to be proud of me, you know. I looked up to him, but the affair and neglecting you...it was wrong. I guess I wanted him to be responsible for the murder, but it wasn't him. He didn't do it. He didn't kill your mother."

"Yeah, I know."

"Good thing I had the case reopened though. It's the least that I could do. And I'm glad I did it. Detective Brent is good. He's gotten a lot further than they had the first time around. He's going to find out what happened to her."

"I hope so. I smiled at Kori. "Thanks, bro."

~***~

"I just heard. Babe, how are you?" Jace asked.

"I'm fine. I've been trying to reach you."

"Reeva was rushed back to the hospital. I've been up here with Yasmine. I promise you when everything is settled---"

"Don't worry about it."

Jace kept talking about Reeva and the drama that was going on in her family concerning her. He never mentioned anything about his father. My guess was that no one had told him. Jace promised to touch base with me that night and with me barely saying much of anything, he was gone again.

"Hey."

I looked up to see Marlo standing there.

"Hey."

"I heard what happened."

"He's dead. And I'm okay."

Marlo stood there.

Grandma had mentioned that she would be moving in that day. Her husband didn't want her at the house or around their kids. And he still didn't know that two of them weren't his.

"Marlo, I'm sorry. I really didn't mean to tell on you. I thought...I didn't mean to mess up your life."

"I messed up my own life. I was wrong. I shouldn't have been sleeping with Corbin in the first place. I mean, what if it had been me there, with Corbin, that night? Instead of Reeva?"

Corbin had been released from jail, and so far, no charges had been filed against him. From what Cassy told me, Corbin had some high-priced lawyer that was telling him all the right things to say.

What did he say to the police? I don't know.

But Cassy said that Corbin made it clear to his lawyer that he would take the fall if it meant keeping her out of jail.

I wondered how long Reeva and Corbin had been fooling around. He was married. She'd been engaged.

Jace told me that Reeva's ex-fiancé hadn't come back to the hospital, after the first day. After he heard that she'd been sleeping with a married man. He told Reeva's mother that he didn't want anything else to do with her.

"I didn't know that he was sleeping with her. He didn't tell me. We'd agreed to only sleep with each other."

"Oh, so his wife wasn't enough, but you thought you would be?" I asked her sarcastically.

Marlo looked at me. "Yes. Anyway, my situation is my own fault. And now, I have to deal with the consequences. In due time, Luis will take me back."

"How can you be so sure?"

"I just am. Luis is angry, but he loves me. He'll forgive me. He's just that type of man. He'll take me back."

"And when he does, you'll never cheat on him again?"

"Now, I didn't say all of that."

What?

"I'll just make sure that I don't get caught next time."

"Marlo! So, after all of this, you're still going to cheat?"

"Probably."

I didn't know what else to say. If Marlo isn't going to be faithful, for god's sake, why not just leave the man alone?

"I know you don't understand, but I'm not you. I need love and stability…and occasional fantasies…with other people. It's how I function. It's what I need. It's what I'll always need."

Cassy walked into the living room. When she saw Marlo, she turned around.

"Cassy?"

She stopped walking.

"I'm sorry. What I did was wrong."

"You damn right it was wrong!" Cassy turned to face her.

"I'm sorry. We're family. I hope one day you can forgive me."

Cassy looked at Marlo, and then she looked at me.

"*Family* wouldn't have done that to me."

And with that, Cassy walked away.

Marlo and I chatted until grandma called for us to help her in the kitchen. All three of us had to help, and she didn't give us a choice. Grandma forced conversation and interaction. She taught me how to make a peach cobbler, and she made Marlo and Cassy peel potatoes together. She was trying to fix it. In her own way, she was trying to clean up the mess. A few times, I caught Cassy smiling at something Marlo said and vice versa. Grandma saw it too. I actually appreciated her just a little bit more for her effort. After about two hours, we all sat down at the table to eat the meal that we'd prepared together.

Dinner was good, and it went as well as grandma could've hoped it would. There were some moments of laughter that I planned to store in my memories forever. That I'd stored deep inside my heart to remember when we were miles apart.

There was no doubt in my mind that the investigation was about to come to an end, and as soon as it was over I planned to leave, and I couldn't be sure when or if I would ever come back again.

After we cleaned up the kitchen, we all went in different directions. I headed into the back bedroom. I'd been alternating between one bag of clothes so that I wouldn't have to take out the other bags already packed and inside my trunk.

I headed to do a load of laundry.

With my clothes in the washing machine, I came back into the room, and I stared at my laptop. I only had a chapter or two left, and though I had plenty to say, I was waiting. I was waiting for the perfect ending.

Harvey's death had been liberating.

I was waking up every day in a brand-new state of mind. I could never repay Kori for what he had given back to me.

Taking Gamma's journal out of my purse, I decided to read a little more of it. I opened it up, and I started to read. By the time I looked up again, hours had gone by, and I'd found out so much about her.

She wasn't as evil as everyone thought she was.

She wasn't as heartless.

She was just broken; just like everyone else.

It made my heart smile to see how much Gamma actually loved her kids; she just didn't know how to show it, and she didn't know how to say it. So, she wrote about it.

She even wrote letters to her children once they died. She would dedicate a whole journal entry to them. Only seven of the ones that had passed away were in this journal. I figured that the other three were probably in a journal that she'd had before.

She told them things that she loved and admired about them. She apologized for things that she had done to them.

I kept reading her journal until I flipped the page and saw that nothing was there.

Is that the end?

Just out of curiosity, I flipped a few more pages, and I'm glad that I did. I found that Gamma had written a few other entries all the way at the back of the journal.

There were three of them.

From the dates, she'd written them over a year ago, and they were to each of her last three living children.

She'd mentioned in her entries that she was writing them because she had a feeling that her time on earth was coming to an end soon. I read the two entries that were written to my great aunts, and then the last one was to grandma.

August 29, 2017

Whinny,

Whinny, if you are readin' this, then I'm dead. Only you would be nosey enough to check underneath the bed. I had to write this just in case I die before you do, which I'm pretty sure I will. My time is comin' soon. I was hard on you. Not 'cause I wanted to be. Not 'cause you did something wrong. It was 'cause of who I knew you were destined to be. You are a fixer. A healer. A caregiver. A fighter. I saw that the minute that I held you in my arms. I'm sorry I wasn't always a good mother. I wanted to be. At first, I tried to be. But life tends to make us who we gotta' be instead. I reckon you'll live for a long time. You have a lot mo' fixin' and lovin' to do. People still need you. I needed you. And when I did, you were there for me. I never said thank you...Thank you, Whinny. I'm gone. I'm sure I'm with your brothers and sisters now, and I'll be waiting for you by the gate. See you in the home in the sky. Oh, and one more thing, Whinny. I never said this either... I'm sorry. And you know why. Goodbye.

Love your mother.

I reread the entry.

I made sure there was nothing else inside of the journal, and then I put it back underneath the mattress so that grandma could find it one day. She needed to read those words from her mother.

I fell asleep that night thinking about mine.

I wondered if Mama was with Gamma in Heaven. I wonder how she felt once she saw her face.

I wish that she had left a journal entry for me.

An explanation. An apology.

For so many things, she never got to tell me why.

Unlike Gamma, she never got to say goodbye.

The next morning, I opened my eyes to a ringing phone. The ringing stopped by the time I picked it up.

Nathaniel.

I hadn't spoken to him in a while, but he always called. He wasn't giving up on me. I laid my phone back down beside me, and it started to ring again.

"Ugh," I groaned.

I thought it Nathaniel, again, but it wasn't.

It was Jace.

"I need you," he said as soon as I picked up the phone.

I sat up. "Is everything okay?"

"Yes, but I need you," he repeated.

"Okay. I'm on my way."

After closing my eyes for a few more minutes, I got up and showered. Thankfully Grandma had already dried and folded my laundry, and she was already up cooking breakfast. I got dressed and carried my clothes, and laptop to the car. I was probably going to be a Jace's for a few days, so I decided to take them with me. I came back into the house and followed the smells into the kitchen.

Uncle Willie was in one of his moods. He was screaming and refusing to take his medicine again. Grandma yelled at him as she fixed me a plate. I laughed at them, ate and then I headed out the door.

About thirty minutes later, I pulled up at Jace's place. I took the engagement ring out of my purse and placed it on my finger.

Jace opened the door as soon as I rang the doorbell. He placed his finger over his lips, indicated that his daughter was asleep, and then he kissed me. He kissed me like I'd never been kissed before, and then he picked me up after shutting the front door. He carried me to his bedroom, and then he did all sorts of nasty things to me. I enjoyed each and every moment of it, knowing that once we were done there was something that I needed to get off my chest.

"I guess you missed me," I exhaled as I snuggled close him. I laid my head on his chest.

"Like crazy. All this is crazy, you know, with Reeva."

"Yeah. I know."

"And with my folks. Our folks."

He was mentioning it.

We hadn't talked about it, and I wasn't sure if anyone had told him.

"It's crazy that your mom and my pops were…"

"I know. I don't know what to say about it. It's weird."

"It's fucked up. I'm disappointed in him. I've always appreciated how much he loved my mother. He taught me everything I know. He taught me how to love a woman. He should've taken his own advice. And of all the rules of the church; hell, he broke a big one. *Thou shall not commit adultery.*"

Jace sounded disgusted. So, was I.

If Mama was going to play the mistress role, she would've been better of continuing to sleep with my father. At least then he would've been around. Maybe then he would've gotten the chance to know and love me.

"I asked him how it happened. He said that it had only gone on for a few weeks. He said it just happened. Nothing just happens. Your mama came to him for help, guidance, and he took advantage of the situation. Plain and simple."

Jace was clearly upset.

"Ma is pissed at him. I don't know what's going to happen with them. I hope this doesn't change us. What they did doesn't have anything to do with us."

I took a deep breath before saying my next words.

"Unless he killed her."

"Who? My dad? Nah, man. He didn't kill nobody."

I sat up to look at him. "How do you know? How can you be sure?"

"Because I know my old man. He may be a liar and a cheat. But he ain't a killer."

"But how can you know that Jace? What if he is?"

"He isn't."

"What if he is?"

"V. He isn't. He didn't kill your mom. I know you wish you knew who did, but my dad didn't kill her."

"Well, they think he did."

"Who?"

"The detective. Kori. She was at the church that night. Your daddy lied about where he was, and no one can prove where he was at the time of the murder. She'd been waiting on him. Obviously, they were supposed to meet up. And then she ends up dead."

Jace got up, and naked, he walked towards the bathroom.

"My father didn't kill your mother, Savannah."

I could tell that Jace was getting offended, but he had to consider the possibility. I'd been thinking about it a lot.

They were sleeping together.

No one saw her alive after she left the church.

No one knows where he was.

Something just didn't add up.

I slid out of bed and headed into the bathroom behind Jace.

Jace got into the shower, but he didn't say a word.

I got into the shower with him.

We both washed in silence. The tension was so thick that you could cut it with a knife. He washed my back, and I washed his.

Jace got out of the shower before me, and I just stood there for a while and allowed the water to hit my face.

I wasn't done with the conversation.

I still had more to say.

Once I came back inside the bedroom, Jace placed my clothes on the bed and a pair of clean panties that I'd left over from another time before.

"Jace?" I said while getting dressed.

"What?"

"All I'm saying is…"

"V. Just let it go. My father isn't a killer. They'll find the killer. It's just not him."

"But how do you know that?"

"Because he isn't."

Jace walked out of the room.

I followed him while putting on my shirt.

He peeked into his daughter's bedroom. She was still asleep. We headed into the kitchen.

"What if she wanted to tell your mother about them? What if she wanted to expose him to the church?"

"Savannah, no. Just let it go, okay? My family is already being shaken up enough from the affair. He doesn't need murder allegations going around too."

"They're already going around Jace. Everyone else checked out. Everyone but him."

"I don't want to talk about that. I want to talk about us. So, considering Reeva's condition, what if I brought Yasmine with me to New York?"

"You still want to go to New York?"

"Of course. Reeva isn't doing good, and Yasmine shouldn't keep seeing her like that. Her parents are going to take care of her. I'll fly Yas home to visit her all the time. We can make it work. I still want to marry you. If you still want to marry me. Do you still want to marry me?" He tapped on the ring on my finger.

I nodded. "Yes, Jace."

"Okay. Well, we will work everything out."

"Unless your father killed my mother."

"Really V? Are we back on that? Really?"

"Yes really. I wouldn't be able to forgive him if he did it. And I don't know how that would affect us."

"He didn't do it, so we don't have to worry about that."

"Why are you defending him?"

"Because he's my father."

"Your father is an adulterous pastor and a killer."

"No, he's not a killer Savannah."

I stared at Jace. "I think he is. I think you know that he is and you're trying to protect him."

Jace walked out of the kitchen, and into the living room. He sat down on the sectional.

"Savannah, please."

"That's it isn't it? You know where he was that night, don't you? You know the truth about what he did?"

"No."

"You're lying."

"I'm not. Are we really going to go back and forth about this? This is childish. Why are we even arguing right now?"

"I want the truth."

"The truth is what it is, but my father isn't a killer."

"Then if not him, then who?"

"I don't know V."

I folded my arms over my chest.

"I'm going to go to the church and ask him. I want to look him in the face and ask him if he killed mama."

"Go ahead. He didn't kill her."

"But what if he did?"

"Damn it, V! He didn't!"

"Yes, he did."

"No, he didn't."

Jace stood up.

There's something here.

Jace knows something about his father. He was protecting him. I could feel it. And I was going to get the truth out of him.

"Why couldn't he have killed her Jace?"

"We both know he's not that type of man."

"We never thought he was a cheater either. We were wrong."

"That's different."

"How?"

"Because cheating isn't murder."

"Maybe your mama did it. Is that it? Did she know about the affair? Did she kill my mama?"

"Please, V. Please. My mama didn't kill anyone either. And don't go to the church accusing her. She's going through enough."

"My mother went through enough! When one of your parents killed her!"

Jace growled. "They didn't kill your mother."

"One of them did! Which one, huh? Which one? Which one of them killed her Jace? Which one? Tell me!"

"Neither! They didn't kill your mother! Your Uncle Willie did! Damn!"

What?

I stopped talking.

Jace looked as though he wished he could take back his words, but he couldn't. I'd heard them. I'd heard them loud and clear.

"What did you say?"

"Your Uncle Willie killed your Mama, V. I was there that night. I was there."

I started to shake my head.

"I came back to your house that night, homecoming night; after I dropped you off. When I got home, ma had fallen asleep watching T.V. Pops wasn't there. And since I still had her car, I showered, changed my clothes and then I went joyriding. After a while, I decided to come back and see you. I couldn't call you because you know how your grandma was about calling the house after nine, but I knew the routine. Park at the top of the road near Mrs. Hilda's house, walk down the driveway, and around the house to your window; just like I'd done so many times before. I had just made it down the driveway when I saw the car lights. And then I heard your mama shouting at someone. I hurried to the side of the house. Your mama was singing, loud, and then I heard the front door open. I knew then that your grandma was still up, and I knew that there was no way in hell that I was gonna' to knock on your window that night. I was anxious for them to go back inside so I could haul ass back up the driveway. And take my ass back home. But then something happened," Jace paused. "I never told anyone. I was there V. I saw your uncle kill your mama."

His words stung my heart, and I felt as though I was on fire. I felt as though I was going to be sick.

"How?"

"You should go talk to your grandma."

"How?" I said again.

"V. Go talk to Whinny. V, I'm sorry."

I felt as though I was *the walking dead.*

I stared at Jace in pain.

"You knew the truth all of this time? And you didn't tell me? You didn't say anything? You knew who killed my mama the whole goddamn time?"

I was disgusted.

Jace started talking, but I couldn't hear him. I couldn't hear anything, but my breaking heart.

I slipped on my shoes and grabbed my purse and keys.

Jace tried to touch me, but I ran from him. I ran out of his house and to my car.

Uncle Willie killed mama?

How?

Why?

"V! V! Savannah!"

I finally allowed myself to hear him as I got into my car, but I didn't respond to him.

There was nothing left to say.

He knew the whole time. And he'd said nothing.

How could he say that he loved me, yet keep something like that from me? For fifteen years, why would he keep such a horrible secret?

I couldn't have gotten back to Clover fast enough. I sped down the gravel towards the house. I got out of the car without shutting the door. It was cold outside, but Grandma was sitting on the porch in a chair.

I rushed towards her.

"Jayceon called me," she said as soon as I approached the porch.

"So, it's true? Please tell me it's not true. Did Uncle Willie kill mama?"

Grandma looked at me, regretfully. "Yes."

I started to whine.

"Sit down."

"No!"

"If you want to hear the truth sit…yo'…ass…down," grandma spaced out her words.

I wanted to hear the truth. All I've ever wanted was the truth, so I sat on the edge of the porch.

"This secret wasn't Jayceon's burden to bear. I never knew that he was out here that night," she started. "Glorianne came home just before midnight. I could hear her singin' as she walked down the gravel. I went outside. She was *pissy* drunk, just like always. I asked her about her car, and she said she didn't know where it was. I asked her how she got home, and she said some man saw her jaywalking and offered her a ride. She said she didn't know him, and that she kept gettin' them lost because she was so drunk. Maybe she was lyin'. The Pastor could've dropped her off. I wouldn't know. We will never know. Anyway, I told her that the way that she drank was ridiculous. She told me to mind my business."

My heart skipped a beat.

"We started arguing. Gamma must've heard the commotion. She came outside. She approached me, and yo' mama as we fussed. Your mama told me to stop trying to run her life when I couldn't run my own husband. Somehow, she knew about yo' grandpa's affair. I never told her that, so I wasn't sure how she found out. I guess that was another reason she looked at marriage as a joke. She knew that her daddy was cheatin' on me and that I didn't plan on leaving him. She called me stupid. I cursed her out, but she was too drunk to care. Gamma tried to reason with her. Glorianne started to sass her. She got so loud. Your grandpa Bobby and Uncle Willie came outside next. I thought you were gonna' come out too. But you never did."

I could hear my phone ringing over and over again from inside my car. It was probably Jace, but I didn't have anything to say to him.

"Gamma was supposed to be trying to calm the situation, but she made it worse. I became the mediator, once Gamma and Glorianne started to call each other names. Gamma fussed at her and pointed her finger in her face. I tried to calm them both down. I told Gamma to relax and let Glorianne go into the house and sleep it off. Maybe things would've gone a little different if she would've listened to me. But she didn't. Next thing I know, Gamma slapped yo' mama so hard that I'm sure folks felt it all the way down in Mississippi," Grandma seemed to be thinking about that night. "And that made everythin' worse. That was the beginning of a tragic end."

Hmmm…

Is that why Gamma said that she was sorry in her journal entry? Was she sorry that she hadn't listened to grandma that night?

"Glorianne had the nerve to slap Gamma back. Why on earth did she do that? I put myself in the middle of them so that nothing else would happen. Willie kept tugging at me. He was trying to pull me away from the arguing. He kept saying: 'Let's go in the house mama'. But I'd shushed him. I was too focused on my daughter and mother at the time. Finally, yo' grandpa decided to help me out, and he grabbed Gamma. I grabbed yo' mama. I tried to talk to her. I tried to calm her down, but she was full of alcohol and irrational. I remember trying to pull her close to me, but she pushed me, hard, and I lost my balance. I fell down. And…"

Grandma paused again.

"Seeing me fall must've done somethin' to your uncle. I think he was tryin' to protect me. Maybe he thought Glorianne was going to attack me. Or maybe seeing me on the ground made him feel as though he'd had enough. You know, sometimes he doesn't take his medication, and he doesn't think clearly. He gets in those moods, even now, where he hates noise, and he stays in his bedroom, where it's quiet and dark. Maybe he just wanted her to be quiet. I don't know. I don't know. All I know is…"

Tears flowed from my eyes.

"Remember those stones that used to be around the porch? The heavy ones. It was about six of them. It all happened so fast. One minute I was on the ground. The next minute, so was yo' mama. He hit Glorianne in the side of her head with one of those big stones. And still holding the stone, he said: 'Shut up, Glorianne! Just shut up!' And then he looked at me and said: 'Okay ma. She's quiet now. Get up. Let's go in the house.' I couldn't move. And Glorianne wasn't moving either."

And there it is.

The ugly truth.

"Yo' grandpa was the first to react. He took the stone from Willie and told him to go inside the house. I waited for Willie to go inside, and then Gamma and I started to panic. I tried to wake Glorianne. I shook her. I spoke to her. Gamma checked for her pulse. She was bleeding. The side of her head was swelling so fast. She wouldn't wake up. She wouldn't open her eyes. I didn't know what else to do. Yo' grandpa had to be the one to say it aloud. 'I think she's dead Whinny. She's dead.' He said. I just didn't want to believe it. I can't be sure of how hard Willie hit her wit' that stone. He's a big man. I can only imagine. And you remember those big stones, don't you? It killed her. He killed her."

I was crying like a baby. And so was she.

There was nothing that I could say. There was nothing that could take the pain away.

Grandma took a deep breath before she continued. "Bobby asked about Willie. You know how he was about him. He always looked out for him. We didn't want him to end up in jail. He isn't right in the head, but they wouldn't have cared. They would've put him in prison with real criminals. He would've died in there. You have to understand. Your uncle is sick. We just wanted to protect him. We'd just lost one child. We couldn't lose him too. We couldn't lose them both in the same night. So, yo' grandpa pulled his little girl from my arms. He picked up his daughter, kissed her forehead, and then he put her on the back of his work truck. I begged him to tell me where he was takin' her, but he wouldn't. He told Gamma and me to clean up the blood and do something with our clothes. He picked up all of the big stones, including the one that Willie killed Glorianne with, and he put them on the back of his truck with her. Lord, if ever I've cried before, that night, I cried like a newborn baby when he drove away with my baby on the back of that truck. I ain't never cried like that before. I was stuck. I couldn't accept what we were doing. I couldn't believe that we were about to cover up my daughter's death. Gamma didn't cry. She just stood there and watched me mourn. And then she forced me to go into the house. She went into the kitchen and came back with a few items, a flashlight, and then she went back outside. I guess she went out there to check for blood, clean it up and whatever else. All I could think about was that my daughter was gone. And that she'd died by the hands of my son. And then you crossed my mind. You should've seen me runnin' to that bedroom to see if you were still asleep. You were. You had your radio on, and yo' homecoming crown still on yo' head. You slept through it all. I could just imagine how you were goin' to

244

feel when you found out she was *gone*, and it broke my heart. And I knew that it was goin' break yours too. I closed your room door back, and after forcing myself to clean myself up, I went upstairs to clean up Willie. I had him to take off all his clothes. He asked if Glorianne and Gamma were still arguing. I didn't answer him. Gamma came upstairs with my clothes, hers, and then asked me for Willie's. Then, she went into the bathroom, and she cut up the clothes into little, tiny pieces. After she finished cutting up the clothes, she took the clothes outside and burned them in one of those tin barrels. The ones that used to be behind the barn. And after putting out the fire, she came back into the house, and little by little, she flushed the remains down the toilet. Gamma told me that she'd cleaned up outside and that there wasn't a trace of blood anywhere. I was numb. She told me that I had to tell Willie what happened, and I had to make sure that he understood that he couldn't say a word about that night to anyone. I went to talk to him. I told Willie what he'd done. He told me that he didn't mean to. That it was an accident. He said that while Glorianne was screaming, he saw a *demon* in her, and a voice in his head told him to shut her up. Do you remember when we read up on schizophrenia that time? Remember what we read about religious delusions as a side effect? Maybe that's what that was. That just had to be what happened. I think he really believed that he saw something else in her. And he that he just wanted her to be quiet. I told him that I didn't want him to end up in jail. I told him that we had to keep what happened to Glorianne a secret. I told him that he could never tell a soul."

I stood up from the porch, but I couldn't walk. My feet felt like cement, and I felt as though I was going to faint.

Still, I stood there.

"Yo' grandpa came home, but he didn't say a word about what he'd done wit' the stones or where he'd taken Glorianne. He asked if we'd handled everything else, and then he blamed me. He blamed me for being so hard on her. He blamed Gamma. He told me that I should've just left her alone. The look in his eyes told me that he would never look at me the same again. I lost my husband, what little I still had of him, the same night that I lost Glorianne. He gave Gamma his clothes to cut, burn and flush them too, and then he went back outside to check the yard. He was out there until the sun came up. I think he was cryin'. And so was I. We all put on smiles for you, that next morning, until you left to babysit, and then that afternoon, the police showed up, and we all had to put on a show again. We had to hurt all over again. It wasn't hard to do because we were all still hurting. I was hurtin' and worried, all at the same time. I was worried about Willie. I wondered if we were gonna' get caught. I wondered if what we'd done would come out. I was just worried. Worried about the person that had dropped off yo' mama that night. I wondered if they would come forward and tell the police that they'd brought her home. But no one ever did. Maybe they weren't from around here. Maybe they were just as drunk as she was and didn't remember her or know who she was. Maybe they were afraid to come forward because they didn't want to be blamed. Or maybe it was Pastor Hall. I don't know. All I know is that no one ever came. No one knew what really happened to her except for us. The police never suspected us. They never assumed that we had anything to do wit' it. Yo' grandpa told me that he'd gotten rid of the tarp that he'd laid her on in the back of his truck, and that they would never find it or the big stones. But no one even bothered to ask us much of anything, other than the basics. Glorianne was gone. The stones were gone. The clothes were gone. And soon, they gave up on the case. They gave up so quickly. They didn't really care about what happened to her. They couldn't care less about what really happened to my baby."

I cared.

"I never forgave myself. None of us did, well, Willie doesn't even remember what happened. I would ask him little things about that night, and he would act confused. One day, I asked him if he remembered what he did, and he argued me up and down that he didn't do anything. He called me a liar and told me that he would never hurt Glorianne. It's like he blocked it out. So, I never mentioned it again. It's better if he doesn't remember it. Unless he's just pretending. But as for me, I will never forget that night. I remember every moment, and every second, that led to the death of my baby."

Walk away, Savannah.

I still couldn't move my feet.

"I can't believe that Jayceon was out here. I can't believe that he has known the truth, all this time. I can't believe he never said anything. Don't blame him, Vana. Blame us. It was us. Not him. He was just a boy. I'm sure he has his reasons for keeping our secret. I sure have mine. She was my daughter. He is my son. My hands were tied. What else was a mother to do? I'm sorry, Vana."

Sorry would never do. Sorry would never be enough.

And blame him...yes, I blamed Jace too!

Just like I blamed her, grandpa, Gamma and most definitely, Uncle Willie. I blamed them all!

They took her from me, and all she could say was sorry.

"I reckon that detective will soon give up. Whatever he could've found linking us to her death, is long gone. Even I don't know what yo' grandpa did with the stones. The clothes with her blood on them are gone. And if he comes around here askin' more questions, thinkin' he knows somethin', I'll push him towards yo' grandpa. He's dead and gone. I'll blame him if I have to. Willie is still alive, and I'll protect him wit' everything that I've got. I've protected him for this long. No sense in stoppin' now."

I stared down at the ground. I imagined that mama was still lying there.

"I'll deny all of this if you decided to tell someone the truth. I wouldn't have a choice but to. Willie can't go to prison. He just can't, Vana."

I was so frustrated that I couldn't get my thoughts together.

I hadn't even thought about what I was going to do with the truth. I didn't know if I was going to tell. I didn't know if I was going to make them pay for what they did to her. The truth is, I couldn't wrap my head around it all. Everything that she'd said was like a blur. It was too much. The truth was too much.

I looked at my car.

I have to get away from here.

Now!

I forced myself to take a step toward my car.

"Savannah."

Grandma never used my real name.

I didn't turn around to face her, so she called my name again.

"Savannah. I'm sorry," she said. I didn't reply. "Forgive me, Vana. Forgive me. Forgive all of us."

I took another step. And then another one.

"Forgive Jayceon."

Fuck him.

I would never be able to forgive him for keeping a secret like this from me. If he loved me, he would've told me. It's just that simple.

"I wish they never reopened the case. I just got you back. You just came back. And now…" Grandma's voice started to crack. "Now…I'll never see you again on this side of Heaven, will I?"

She knew it. She knew that once I was gone, I would never come back here. This wasn't my home. There was nothing left here for me.

It seemed like forever, but finally, I made it to my car.

"My sweet girl, I love you. Grandma has always loved you."

That's the first time she's ever said those words.

And it was the first and last time that I would ever hear them from her.

I was crying, and I could tell that she was too.

"Goodbye grandma," I mumbled between my tears.

"Goodbye, Savannah."

I got into my car, and through blurry eyes, I took one last look at her. It was the last time I would ever see her face. It was the last memory I would ever have of her.

She sat there as I started to back away. She didn't wave. She didn't move. She just sat there, looking at me. I saw Marlo and Cassy come onto the porch and they looked at her and then looked towards my car. Marlo held up her hand as if she was saying goodbye. Cassy walked over to hug grandma.

I glanced up to the top of the house to see Uncle Willie standing in the window. He was waving at me. The sight of him caused me to press harder on the gas.

Murderer!

Once I reached the dirt road, I just sat there. I looked down the driveway at the house.

The house of secrets.

The house of lies.

The house where everyone has something to hide.

And the house where my mama died.

My phone started to ring, and quickly, I glanced down at it.

Jace called, and then he hung up and called again.

I ignored him and switched the car from reverse into drive, and then I took off his ring.

I stared at it and all of its beauty, and then I tossed it out the window just as I pressed on the gas. From this point on, everyone in Clover, South Carolina, only exists in my past.

~***~

SEVEN MONTHS LATER

"Savannah, it's always a pleasure to see to you. Only this time, instead of one of your authors being in the hot seat, it's you."

I smiled at the interviewer.

My book *Southern Secrets* was soon to be released. It had been picked up by the same publishing company that I used to work for, and they had me doing a few interviews to promote my upcoming book.

"It's good to see you too, Essa."

"And you're glowing. Look at that baby bump!"

I was pregnant; with Jace's baby.

But he would never know it.

After leaving Clover, I was a mess. I didn't know what to do with what I'd found out. I wasn't sure what I could do. I went back and forth with myself, but the truth was too much trouble. If I told the truth, grandma and Uncle Willie could end up in jail.

So, I said nothing.

I didn't say anything, to anyone.

I came back to New York, and Nathaniel helped me put the pieces of my life back together. A month after being back in New York, I found out that I was pregnant. Nathaniel knew that the baby wasn't his. He knew that I was pregnant with Jace's child, but he was willing to love *it* and take care of it as if the child was his own. I told him that Jace didn't want anything to do with the baby. I lied. I never told Jace I was pregnant. I didn't tell him about his child. And I never would.

I never wanted to speak to him again.

Never in a million years did I think I would be doing to my child, the exact thing that mama had done to me, but it was the only way.

This is how it has to be.

I was almost due, but two months ago, Nathaniel and I got remarried. I was Mrs. Smith again, and I was proud of it.

"Yes. This baby caught my husband and me by surprise. I can't wait to meet my precious baby boy." I made sure not to say how many months I was on national T.V. just in case Jace was watching.

"Well, he's going to have a mother who is also a best-selling author, that's for sure! Honey, I read this advanced copy, and this book is…SCANDALOUS! There are so many lies, so many secrets, and so much deception in this book! The twists and turns kept me wanting to read more!"

"Well, then my job is done. Really though, I'm so proud of this book. And believe it or not, it didn't take me long to write it. I used to look at author's with a side-eye when they would tell me stories about how fast they wrote their novels. But it can definitely be done with a little inspiration. My trip home to the South definitely inspired me."

It'd done more than inspire me.

Sheriff Kori, my brother, called me shortly after I left South Carolina. He said that the detective had reached a dead end. It took some digging, but at the presumed time of mama's death, he was able to dig up some footage from years ago of the Pastor's car; far away from where mama's body was found. With him in the clear, Detective Brent was stuck and looking for other possible suspects.

I told Kori to close the case. I told him to shut it down. I told him if it was in his power, just close it and let it be. To let me move on and to let mama rest in peace. Kori said that he take care of it, and after he apologized, he asked me to stay in touch. I told him I would, but I had no plans on speaking to him again. For my sanity, I had to forget about him too.

Months ago, after the never-ending phone calls from Marlo and Jace, I changed my phone number.

Jace.

I never answered any of his phone calls, but I'd read every last text message that he'd sent and listened to every single voicemail that he left.

The very last voicemail he left was:

"V, I just have to tell you this. I didn't say anything because I knew that the truth would hurt you. In my own way, I was protecting you. You may not understand it, but I was. Your mama was gone. And had I said something, you would've lost your grandma, your grandpa, Gamma, and your uncle too. I just couldn't do that to you. I couldn't cause you any more pain than what you were already going through. I couldn't leave you all alone. With no one. You had me, but that wouldn't have been enough. I thought I was doing what was best for you. You may never understand it, but that's love. To keep that secret, to try to protect you from the truth was the only thing that I knew to do. Because I love you V. I almost had you back. We almost had it all. We almost had forever. I guess forever just wasn't in the cards for us. Now, it's just Yasmine and me. I love you V. And I always will. I know it won't just be another fifteen years; I know that you're gone forever this time. At least this time I can say goodbye. Goodbye Savannah."

I'd listened to that voicemail at least twenty times. I cried every single time, and I cried as I changed my phone number.

I hadn't heard from any of them since.

And I wouldn't hear from any of them ever again.

I did check into Corbin and Cassy. Cassy turned herself in. I don't know why. I don't know if the lawyer convinced them that she would be easier to get off, considering the circumstances, but she'd been booked for 'aggravated assault'. That's it. No attempted murder or anything. That was her only charge. It said that she'd been released on bail.

I also checked into Marlo and Luis. On social media, I saw them in a picture together. They were kissing and seemed to be working through their problems. I know that she said she was still going to fool around on him, but I was hoping that she had a change of heart. After it came out that Cassy was the one who hit Reeva with the bat, I hope that Marlo realized that she needed to stay the hell away from other people's husbands' and focus on her own.

I remember after viewing Marlo's social media page, I blocked everyone from the South. I didn't want them to keep up with my life, and I didn't want to keep up with theirs.

I didn't even want to keep up with my father either. I decided that I didn't need him in my life. I no longer *needed* him to love me.

It had taken tons of hours in therapy, but I was getting through my issues. I was getting back to my happy place. I was getting back to where I was long before my visit to the South.

Now, my only concern was my career, my happiness, Nathaniel and my baby. Sure, keeping the baby a secret from Jace was wrong, but he'd kept an enormous secret from me. He kept the truth from me, for fifteen years. And now I was going to keep the truth from him.

Forever.

Karma.

"So, tell me something. I'm a Northern Girl, so I wouldn't know, but are there really that many *Secrets of the South*?" The interviewer asked, interrupting my thoughts.

I nodded at her, and then I exhaled.

"Honey, yes. Forget 'Southern Charm'. It's more like...*Southern Hell*. The only good thing about the South is that there's always a story to tell."

And finally, I told mine.

****

THE END

For autographed paperbacks visit: www.authorbmhardin.com

To contact: E-mail: bmhardinbooks@gmail.com

www.ingramcontent.com/pod-product-compliance
Lightning Source LLC
Chambersburg PA
CBHW032028120726
47901CB00002BA/494